A SOLDIER'S
Seduction

EM BROWN

A Soldier's Seduction

Copyright © 2009 by Em Brown

To My Husband

A SOLDIER'S
Seduction

Chapter One

Eying herself in the mirror to see that all the elements of her police outfit were in place, from the silver badge to the black cap, Pauline San Martin told herself that even though she was dressed for a striptease, even though she had received a pink slip before she had started her new job, and even though her boyfriend had dumped her just three weeks ago, life could be worse. Of course, for someone who had her health, a roof over her head – at least for now – and most of her life still ahead of her, life could be *a lot* worse.

"It can *always* be worse," her roommate, Crystal, had whined. "But just because I should be grateful that I'm not dying of starvation in some impoverished Third World country doesn't mean I should be happy about our situation. I could really use a new pair of Uggs for the winter."

Pauline looked down at her black over-the-knee boots that accompanied her faux leather miniskirt and fur-lined handcuffs. Unlike the rest of her outfit, which was purchased at a secondhand costume shop, the boots were her own clothing and made of genuine leather. They were perhaps the most expensive wardrobe item she owned, and unless her job prospects changed, she was going to have to make this pair last a long time.

She looked hot. Not supermodel-hot, for she wasn't one of those women who weighed a hundred and ten pounds despite their six-foot height and D-size boobs. With her almond eyes and long lashes, she was decent-looking, but was not a knockout. She had a trim but not skinny figure, a little wide in the hips, tall for someone who was part Filipina, shoulders that never required shoulder pads, and long hair that seemed neither brown nor black but a nondescript middling color that Crystal said needed only some highlights to make interesting. But if Caleb could see her now, maybe he wouldn't have been so quick to dump her.

Or maybe he would. His new girlfriend was a blond bombshell with legs that went on forever. And she drove a sleek silver BMW convertible. There was no way Pauline, with her little Toyota Tercel, could compete with that.

And though she and Caleb had only been dating for two months, she had had the feeling that Miss Blond Bombshell hadn't been a recent find. So it was just as well that Caleb had dumped her rather than continue to two-time her.

"You've got to stop dating those bad-boy types," Crystal had told her. "Women like to think they're that special someone who can turn a bad boy good, but the truth is a bad boy is always a bad boy."

"It's worse than that. I was dating him for his motorcycle," Pauline had quipped.

And it was partly true. Caleb had a very nice bike. When he had pulled up on his Harley with his I-know-I-can-get-you-in-bed-with-just-my-smile smirk, looking like James Dean or Marlon Brando, she had fallen for him, and knew it wasn't going to take more than two or three dates to go from first base to home.

"How did I let you talk me into this?" Crystal groaned, pulling uncomfortably at her short nurse's outfit.

She was standing with Pauline in the women's room of the Visitor Center at the Brandywine Battlefield Historic Site in

Chadds Ford, Pennsylvania, just an hour's drive from Philadelphia.

"You realize if anyone finds out we did this, we're never going to get jobs as teachers.

They won't let us near kids," Crystal added.

"This is easy money," Pauline reminded her, turning around to see that her own miniskirt barely covered her butt cheeks and the black thong underneath. "And the landlord told me if we're late on our rent for the third time, we're out of there."

"You'd think that someone with our backgrounds – our educations and all the goddamn loans we took out to get where we are – you'd think we wouldn't have to resort to this kind of work."

"It's a striptease, Crystal, not prostitution."

"And why are we doing this here? This is such a funky place."

"You've never been here? I think it's a really cool place. It's beautiful and loaded with history."

"Why don't these guys go to a club?" Crystal persisted.

Pauline dabbed at her lipstick – the only makeup she tended to wear. "Because it's a surprise party for the groom-to-be."

"What if there are kids and families around? We could get caught for indecent exposure."

"The park will be closed."

"What about our bouncer?"

"He's doing the reenactment, too. I'll go first. You can be the surprise second act. And remember my stage name is Miss Lipps. Pauline just doesn't cut it."

When she was a girl, she had always given herself

imaginary names. Names that were a lot more romantic and feminine than Pauline. She wished she could have been born a Charlotte, Marianne, or Brianna. But her father had wanted to name his firstborn after her grandfather, and so Pauline it was.

"All right," Crystal grumbled. "I'm just gonna do my hair and I'll meet you outside."

Pauline wanted to tell her friend that the men wouldn't be looking at her hair, but she decided not to say anything. Putting on a trench coat that made her feel like a bank robber, she headed back out into the lobby of the Visitor Center.

She thought about what Crystal had said and had to agree that she never thought she would come to this. She had gotten herself through college, worked for Teach for America, gotten a master's degree in education, and tonight she was going to be a stripper. Someone hadn't gotten the memo about how her career was supposed to turn out. She was supposed to be a high school history teacher – although she would have been happy teaching almost anything, history was where her heart lay.

And there was no way she was going back to live with her mom and dad in Connecticut, even though she knew many of her generation had taken that route. All three of her brothers were living on their own, making it work. She didn't want to be the only one who had to crawl back to mom and dad.

Past the cash register and the gift shop, the small museum within the Center had a collection of items dating back to the American Revolution: uniforms, weapons, and even jewelry. Pauline studied a silver pocketwatch with the name *Bradford* engraved upon the inside cover. The note next to the watch read "Property of British Brigadier General Stephen Bradford, fell at the Battle of Monmouth Courthouse, 1778."

The Visitor Center was closing soon, so Pauline decided to take a walk outside. Less crowded than many other parks, there was serenity among the rolling hills and lush trees of Brandywine Battlefield. Pauline would have liked to see the reenactment of what was one of the largest single-day battles in the American War of Independence. The Battle of Brandywine actually occurred 232 years ago almost to the day on September 11, 1777. As she walked up one of the hills, she tried to imagine whose footsteps might have tread where she now walked.

George Washington? Alexander Hamilton? And what would it have felt like to be…

Before she could finish her thought, she tripped over the roots of a tree and tumbled headfirst down the hill. The world went black.

Chapter Two

Through the darkness, the steady beating of her heart seemed to amplify the throbbing ache in her head. Pauline opened one eye. The hill hadn't been that steep, yet she felt as if she had fallen from the rooftop of the Visitor Center. With a groan, she pushed herself onto her knees and waited for the world to stop whirling. She examined herself. No broken bones. No torn clothing. Just a few scratches on her arms and thighs and a general soreness throughout her body.

She brushed the dirt from her leather skirt.

The striptease!

Scrambling to her feet, Pauline glanced at her watch. 5:33 PM. She was only a few minutes late. Crystal was probably wondering where she was. Trying to shake off the fog around her head, Pauline headed in the direction of the reenactment site, where the men were supposed to be waiting. Oddly, it seemed darker than she remembered. Darker than it should be for 5:33 PM.

Coming upon a clearing, she saw a group of men in red uniforms sitting on the ground about a campfire. Pauline looked for Crystal. Was she still in the Visitor Center? Had she chickened out? Well, it didn't matter. Taking a deep breath, Pauline shed her coat and pushed aside the shrubbery. If she was going to do this, she might as well make it good and hope that these guys were good tippers.

"So I've been told someone here has been a bad, bad boy,"

Pauline said as she stepped up to the men, swirling a pair of fake handcuffs about her finger.

A few reached immediately for their weapons while others stared at her with a strange, almost dazed, look of surprise.

"Which one of you bad boys is Evan Armstrong, the groom-to-be?" Pauline asked as she bent at the waist to look into their faces, allowing them a deep look at her cleavage. "I've got a warrant for your arrest."

No one spoke. They simply stared. Damn. She should have asked the bouncer what the groom looked like. Maybe he was shy. But you'd think his buddies who arranged the striptease would point him out.

"All right, maybe I'll have to interrogate all of you boys," Pauline improvised as she moved into the center of their semicircle. She expected a lot of hoopla around her announcement, but these guys seemed...tired. Maybe they were all shy and just needed to be warmed up.

"First, let me introduce you to my partners," she said and ripped open her shirt. The

Velcro came apart easily. No wardrobe malfunction here.

The eyes of the men grew wide in shock, as if they had never seen a woman in a bra before. Pauline half wondered if they were Amish, they looked so stricken. She let her shirt slide off her arms and ran her fingers over the tops of her breasts, which were enhanced by her black padded push-up bra. She had even applied a lotion that made her breasts gleam in the light of the

fire.

"You boys like my partners?" Pauline asked with a coy smile, cupping her breasts higher with her hands and blowing each orb a kiss.

A few mouths dropped open. Was she going too fast? Should she be pacing herself more?

Pauline glanced through the trees for Crystal, but her roommate was nowhere in sight.

* * * *

"It will have to be amputated," the doctor said grimly, "or the infection will spread."

Captain Kerry Bradford stared at the ashen face of the soldier lying on the makeshift operating table in the Old Kent Meeting House, where the wounded from the battle five days ago had been brought. Grapeshot had mangled the soldier's leg into a bloody mess of burnt flesh. Having served nearly a decade in the service of His Majesty's Army, Bradford thought he would be accustomed to the gruesomeness of battle, and he could tolerate almost anything in the thick of battle, but away from the smoke and gunfire, he found it harder to stomach the pain his men had to endure.

"He appears to have taken the fire at close range," the doctor noted.

Bradford felt the muscle along his jaw tighten. "Yes. A company of the rebels had run up a white flag. We went out to receive it, and they opened fire upon us."

"How cowardly!"

"I lost two of my men." Bradford looked at the doctor. "I have no wish to lose a third."

The solider on the table groaned. Bradford eyed the cutting instrument held by the doctor's assistant.

"Some brandy first for my man," Bradford directed.

The doctor hesitated. "As you know, Captain, brandy is

A SOLDIER'S SEDUCTIONS

reserved for officers."

Bradford stared down the surgeon. "I said some brandy, Doctor."

The doctor hesitated, then gestured for one of his assistants.

"Captain Bradford!"

It was Jeremy Townsend, with a number of other young men who had been pressed into service on the day of the battle.

"Will you tell us again of how you won the day?" one of the lads asked.

Bradford looked down at the boy – probably no more than six and ten years of age – and recalled a time when he himself had been as eager and excited to learn about battles. Now, at nearly thirty, the captain felt old. Perhaps because the battle had been a grueling one. Perhaps because they had marched seventeen miles to reach Brandywine. Perhaps it was because he felt this revolution, as the colonists termed it, had merely started, and the end was not yet in sight.

Accustomed to being the center of attention, especially among young men impressed by his carriage and his regimentals, Bradford indulged them and told them of how Sir William Howe, commander-in-chief of His Majesty's Army, had split the army in two. General Kynphausen had taken a force of five thousand men and engaged the rebel army at Chadds Ford. It was a risky move on the part of Sir William, but the American commander-in-chief was fooled into thinking Kynphausen's men comprised the whole of the British army. The rebel army became disoriented as the British forces fired upon them from the front and the rear.

"Ah, did the rebels flee then?"

"Quite briskly, but at about thirty minutes past seven, we were attacked by troops of Washington, who had circled round north and west of Dilworth Crossroads, and even presented a cavalry charge to our surprise, but they could not hold against our troops and fled in some panic toward Chester."

"Will you give chase? Will you march to Philadelphia? What will happen next?" came the litany of questions.

"Another day," Bradford said. The armies had already attempted to reprise the battle yesterday. The British had divided themselves into three columns, and it had appeared that Washington had caught himself on soft ground. But the skies had opened up and a deluge of rain put an end to the battle.

"You best be off, lads, for it is nearly curfew," Bradford advised the boys. "If you tarry longer, you will have to stay the night."

The young men seemed slightly disappointed but did as told. He himself left the Old Meeting House and headed back toward his camp. A young man on horseback rode by.

"Kerry!"

"Captain André," Bradford greeted the handsome young man. He and Captain John André had entered His Majesty's Army in the same year and both had served in Canada.

"Dear friend, I am glad to see you have emerged unscathed, for I understand you to have led a charge against the American artillery."

"Aye, the 84th Foot had lost their captain and intended to retreat."

"We will take Philadelphia in short order, I am sure of it. I can hardly wait for the welcome we are sure to receive –

especially among the lovely ladies of that city."

With his charm, John would no doubt receive a warm welcome indeed from the women of Philadelphia. Fluent in many languages and adept at the arts and verse, John was a favorite in almost any society they had come across.

"Captain Bradford! Captain Bradford!"

Bradford turned to see his lieutenant, James Willoughby, running up to him. The young man's boyish face was flushed.

"Captain, there is something most strange occurring in our encampment," Lieutenant Willoughby said.

Something was wrong. Bradford could sense it from the heightened pitch in his lieutenant's voice.

"What is it?"

"It be – it be a woman – I think."

Bradford raised a brow. "You *think*?"

"An Injun. Half mad, I believe."

"Is she threatening our troops?"

"I – I don't know."

Bradford was tempted to tell the lieutenant that surely the young officer could handle the matter himself, but something was obviously amiss, for Willoughby was a sensible man – or had been till now.

"Very well, I will attend to this." He bid John adieu followed Willoughby to where his troops had made camp. "Is this woman armed?"

"I think not, but she makes threats and accusations in a strange tongue, using mostly English words – I gather. I find it difficult to comprehend all that she speaks."

As I do with all that you currently speak, Bradford could not help but think to himself.

They walked past the other regiment of light dragoons to

19

their own company.

"There," directed Lieutenant Willoughby. "There be the Injun."

Bradford looked past the trees and the throng of men gathered to where there was, indeed, the silhouette of a woman. A *naked* woman. Or nearly naked. She had on an odd corset – one that barely covered her bosom and left her midsection bare, a short skirt, and boots that must have belonged to a man, though they seemed to mold and encase her legs as if they had been made for a woman. Bradford had seen the native women of the Americas, but none dressed as wantonly as this one.

Nor *moved* as wantonly. This woman was caressing herself in the most hedonistic manner. He watched as she rolled her hips in a shockingly suggestive way. Her hands went down her backside, and she patted one buttock with a teasing smile. Then she bent down slowly, sliding her hands down her boots, until – dear God – one could view the bottom of her arse peeking from beneath her skirt. She was on her knees, crawling about like a cat, pushing her bosom into the face of a soldier. Now lying on her back, one leg stretched to the sky, a hand trailing the inside of her thigh.

"Dear bodkins," he heard Willoughby murmur.

Bradford felt warm – and it wasn't due to the summer heat that lingered in the air even after the sun went down.

The woman stood back on her feet and, with a flash of the hands, ripped her skirt off to reveal…

Bradford pushed aside the men to reach her.

"Desist!"

* * * *

Finally, the men were getting into it, Pauline thought with relief. She noticed their faces were animated, and some wore broad grins. She had thought them a tough crowd, and the eerie silence that had initially greeted her had shaken her confidence. But as she made her way through her routine and saw the lust growing in their eyes, she found herself reveling a little in all the attention. Perhaps she had a natural talent for stripping?

The men had definitely been tired – tired from the reenactment and tired from being baked under the sun while wearing their uniforms and battle gear. It was amazing how realistic everyone was. Almost all had the stubble of a beard coming in as if they hadn't shaved in the morning. Some even had 'battle wounds.' But the men had finally come alive, hollering and cheering her on. The only part that bothered Pauline was that no one was tipping yet.

And Crystal was still nowhere in sight. How long did she plan on waiting?

"Desist!"

Pauline stood, a little stunned at her own audacity in ripping off the skirt. Now she stood before dozens – had the crowd grown in size? – with only her bra, thong, and boots. There was bound to be some tipping now. She waved her skirt above head and threw it at a soldier in front of her.

"Desist!"

The stern voice cut through the ribaldry, and the next thing she knew, a man in a scarlet uniform had grabbed her by the arm and was dragging her out of the circle of soldiers.

"Hey, let go!" Pauline exclaimed. "I'm not done yet."

"You most certainly are, madam," he replied and thrust her

into a tent.

Pauline stumbled away from him. Was he the director of the park? His costume seemed more ornate than the others. She noticed his coat had exquisite gold epaulets and brass buttons. He also sported a gorget at the throat, a purple sash across the waist, and a sword encased in a gold-tipped sheath. He didn't look like a park director. If it weren't for the frown on his face, she would have said he was quite attractive. Surprisingly, he didn't seem effeminate in his getup with his powdered hair rolled above his ears and his smartly tied cravat billowing beneath his neck. He looked...regal.

"Look, I'm just doing my job," she told him as she rubbed her arm where he had grabbed her.

His cornflower blue eyes narrowed. "What job?"

"A little pre-nup entertainment. Evan's friends set it up."

"Evan? Who is Evan?"

"Don't you know?" Pauline returned, perturbed by his tone. And why did he persist in speaking with an English accent?

"Evan Armstrong."

"Madam, I know no Evan Armstrong." He frowned as he glanced at her, then quickly glanced away as if looking at her was inappropriate. He removed his coat. "Put this on."

Pauline stared at the coat. Was he serious?

"That's all right," dismissed Pauline. She wanted to finish her job so that she could get paid.

"Madam, it was *not* a request."

The guy was serious. He wasn't even looking at her directly but kept his eyes averted to the side. Wow. *He is some prude,* Pauline thought to herself. His unease was contagious. She would have felt more comfortable completely naked in front of the dozen or so men outside than half naked inside the tent with this guy.

Pauline took the coat from him and put it on. The man looked painfully relieved. She wondered if she was going to be in trouble. Maybe Evan's friends hadn't received proper authorization for their surprise party. Would this stick-in-the-mud report her to the police?

"Look," said Pauline, "I just want to get paid, then me and my friend will be out of here."

He eyed her solemnly. "You have a cohort?"

"Yeah, we were supposed to do this together, but I'm not sure where she's at right now. I should probably go look for her. Something might have happened to her."

She moved to exit the tent, but he blocked her way. She suddenly wondered why the bouncer wasn't here with her. Perhaps he had not been part of the crowd. Was he with Crystal?

"You may search for your friend later," he told her, "but I must impress upon you, madam, that such a display as you have conducted is not allowed in my company."

Pauline stared at him. "Huh?"

"I would that you confine your appeals to where the other women of your trade have made camp."

"Are you joking?"

He was joking. Playing the part of a British officer. Why he was pulling her chain, Pauline wasn't sure.

"I trust I have made myself clear?" he asked. "You seem to have some knowledge of the English language."

Pauline laughed. "Okay, this is kind of weird, but I get you. You're very good. The accent is top-notch. Method acting?"

The man stared at her as if gibberish had fallen from her

lips. "Madam, this is no jest."

"Did Crystal put you up to this? Am I on some like candid-camera show?" Pauline looked about her for some telltale sign that a ruse was being perpetrated upon her, but the tent was sparsely furnished, with only a cot, a table, and a chair.

"What…of what do you speak?" he asked.

"You're kinda cute with that English accent," teased Pauline, sauntering a little closer to him. It wasn't like her to be this forward with a guy, but if he was going to persist in this ridiculous playacting, she would play her part. "You want a private performance? Cost you twenty bucks."

She reached out to touch his chest, but he gripped her wrist. Pauline looked up at him, and her breath caught as she realized how close she was to him. Uncomfortably close. Yet it was electrifying. She could feel every one of his fingers wrapped about her. As she gazed into his eyes – they seemed to be composed of hundreds of grayish blue crystals – she felt an overwhelming desire to be kissed by him. His frown gave way to an intense stare, his grip relaxing ever so faintly. He seemed to lean in toward her, making the breath catch in her throat.

And just as suddenly, he pulled away. "Lieutenant Willoughby!"

A younger man, also in officer uniform, appeared. This one had clear blue eyes set in baby-boy features.

"Captain Bradford?" the lieutenant inquired.

"Please escort Miss…Miss …"

"Lipps."

"Miss Lipps to where the women have made camp," the captain instructed.

He handed Pauline to the other man. The captain was

unsettled, she could tell, but why? He was the strangest fellow she had ever met. She wanted to say something to the man but could not find the words, so she followed "Lieutenant Willoughby" out of the tent. Maybe now she would finally get paid.

* * * *

Bradford watched the strange woman and Lieutenant Willoughby exit the tent. Only in taverns with drunken whores had he ever come across a woman so brazen or disconcerting. He could not shake the odd feeling that had passed between them when she had attempted to touch his chest. As if he knew her, or had known her.

But that was impossible. He would have remembered her. She was tall for an Indian – tall for any woman. Her body was dark and strong like that of an Indian woman, and yet there was something unique and rare in her features that was unlike the other natives he had seen. She was a little broad, as if she had been well nourished for most of her life, and appeared much healthier than the other strumpets who followed the British army. Her English wanted refinement, and he could not place her accent. It was neither Welsh nor Scottish nor even Irish.

The woman was not wise. Her wanton behavior before an entire company of men invited trouble. She was fortunate not to have been molested or harmed. He would have assigned her recklessness to gin, but aside from her brashness and odd speech, she did not appear inebriated. Where had she come from? Was her bawdy act one that she performed at country fairs? His fellow officers, many of whom made no mystery of which strumpets they favored, would surely have mentioned her had they seen her before.

Miss Lipps. That was the name she had given him. An odd name for an odd woman.

Visions of her bare buttocks flashed in his mind, and Bradford felt his face color though he was entirely alone in his tent. Her arse had a nice curvature to it. A little more plump than those he had occasion to see on women. And it was not her naked form that he found wanton but the manner in which she moved, the way her hands caressed her body. He felt the blood coursing in his groin. Where had she learned to move like that?

He shook his head. He had other matters to attend to, but he had the feeling that he had not seen the last of the strange woman.

Chapter Three

Clutching her police outfit to her chest, Pauline barreled through the bushes and past the trees. She had given Lieutenant Willoughby the slip while a woman playing a prostitute had distracted him with a proposition. When had prostitutes become part of the reenactment? The women had looked so real – many of them scrawny, petite, and haggard. Something weird was going on, Pauline determined as she made her way back to the Visitor Center. She wondered if Crystal had gotten waylaid as well.

By the position of the moon in the sky, Pauline could tell that it was later than she had expected. She glanced at her watch. Still 5:33. That wasn't right. She had just gotten a new watch battery last week. It was then she realized she was still wearing the captain's coat and had forgotten her own trench coat somewhere. She'd have to sort the coats out later. Right now she just wanted to make her way back to the Visitor Center and the parking lot. Her cell was in her car, and she could try to call Crystal. She almost felt like calling the police. These people were a little spooky.

Had she taken a wrong turn? Where had the Visitor Center gone? Climbing up the knoll she thought she had fallen down, Pauline looked about and saw only a clearing with…

Bodies? Dozens of them. Lying on the ground like logs after a forest clearing.

A shiver like the touch of a ghostly hand went up her spine. Shaking it off, Pauline stumbled down the knoll and approached the closest body.

"Hello?" she asked. It was probably a dummy, but why did she feel like something was about to jump out at her?

She stepped gingerly toward the body. Maybe this was a full-scale reenactment of the battle. The body faced away from her. In the light of the moon, she could tell it wore the uniform of a soldier. She nudged it with her foot. Nudged it harder. Then walked warily to the front of it.

She stifled a scream. Hair clung to its face with what appeared to be blood. The mouth hung open as if in the middle of an agonized groan. Part of the face looked as if it had been blasted off, the white of the jawbone protruding through the flesh.

Backing away, she fell over another body. She didn't want to see its face, but she had to.

This one at least had its features intact, but the eyes were open, staring lifelessly up at the stars. The eyes. They were too real.

But it couldn't be real. She gave it one hard push. It had to be a dummy. A very realistic mannequin. She poked it in the face and felt the soft give of flesh.

Then she heard a moan that made her skin crawl. It came from another mannequin. Pauline walked over to it and poked it. It was *warm*. Her heart hammered in her ears. Should she turn it over? What were the chances it was real? Wasn't it curiosity that killed the cat? Or in this case, the part-time stripper?

It moaned again. Biting down on her lower lip, Pauline rolled the heavy mass onto its back. A large black stain had soaked through the man's coat. She unbuttoned the coat and pulled it open to reveal an even larger stain on the waistcoat, which she also unbuttoned. The man's shirt was sodden with a slick, warm liquid. She ripped it open to reveal the wound. It was as if something had sliced into him. Something like a bayonet.

"Oh God, oh God," Pauline muttered to herself. This man was real. His wound was real.

Somehow it was real.

"We need to get you to a hospital," she said to the man, hoping she hadn't worsened his injury by rolling him over.

"Somebody help!" she called into the night. "Help! I need 9-1-1!"

But nothing greeted her ears. Not the sound of wind moving through the trees. Not crickets. Nothing.

She scrambled to the next nearest body and ripped off the shirt. It wasn't easy getting at the shirt, but she needed it to bind the wound and stanch the loss of blood. Even in the faint moonlight, she could tell the soldier was pale. Soldier. Actor. Whatever he was.

In between cries for help that went unanswered, she did her best to wrap the shirt around the man's ribs and applied pressure. How could she get the women and men in the reenactment to come to her aid? Should she try to drag the body to them?

"Help!" she cried again. Though her hands were slippery with blood, she felt for the man's pulse. It was so weak, she barely found it. She would have to leave him and go on foot to find help.

"Hold on, just hold on," she told him, slapping him a few times on the cheek. "I'm going to get help. Just stay with me a little longer. Stay with me."

She was so focused on the man before her, she barely

noticed the orange glow until it was upon her. Whirling around, she found herself looking up at the familiar forms of Captain Bradford and Lieutenant Willoughby on their horses.

"This man's hurt," she pleaded.

The captain dismounted and set down his lantern. He knelt beside her to examine the wounded man. He turned to Lieutenant Willoughby. "We best get him to the Meeting House. He is near dead."

"Meeting House?" Pauline exclaimed. "We need to get him to the hospital! Or get an ambulance here. You got a cell phone?"

"Pardon?"

"A cell phone."

"A what?"

"A *cell phone*. What are you, Amish?"

Still the confused look.

"Never mind. We should just get him to a hospital. I think the nearest one is Chester County."

She received a perplexed stare.

"There is no hospital nearby," Captain Bradford told her. "Our doctors are quite capable."

"You have doctors on-site?" she asked with relief. The idea of doctors hanging around a reenactment was strange, but then, sports games usually had medical personnel around, and maybe the reenactment was not unlike a football game.

She watched as the captain and lieutenant eased the injured man onto one of the horses. Lieutenant Willoughby took the reins and led him back the way they had come, leaving her alone with Captain Bradford and his horse.

"There might be others." Pauline spoke her realization aloud as she went to the next body. This one looked real as well.

The captain knelt before the body and searched for a pulse, then rose to his feet. He looked at her solemnly and shook his head.

"No," Pauline said. "It doesn't make any sense. He's pretending. It's an act."

Like maybe this was all just part of a movie set, the latest Hollywood epic. Pauline put her ear to the body's chest to listen to the heartbeat. Not finding one, she pulled up the eyelids, hoping to jar the man back to life so that he could leap to his feet and have a good laugh at her expense, at how he had fooled her into thinking he was dead.

"Miss Lipps."

Ignoring the sympathy in his tone, Pauline tried again for a pulse. "Maybe he just needs CPR. I took a first-aid class long time ago in high school. Do you know...?"

The look in his face provided the answer.

"There is nothing more that can be done for him." He took her gently but firmly by the elbow and pulled her to her feet.

Pauline stared at the lifeless body on the ground, then jerked her elbow out of his grip. She was trembling all over. Maybe they were part of a sadistic group of crazy people involved in a twisted, gruesome version of *Fight Club*, though something in the captain's eyes – was it pity? – suggested otherwise.

"I'm going to find other help," Pauline persisted.

He grabbed her arm before she could leave. "You are not permitted to leave."

Pauline raised an eyebrow, outwardly calm but churning inside. "Why?"

"Because Sir William Howe has imposed a curfew."

"Sir William Howe? As in Major General Howe?"

"Be there any other?"

The man was trying her patience. "Look, I already said you were good. But I think it's time we dropped the charade. What if there are others here who are hurt?"

"We have combed the fields for survivors of both armies and will finish burying the last of the dead. And to what charade do you refer?"

"This!" replied Pauline, flinging an arm toward the field before them. "You. It's like you believe you're in the frickin' Battle of Brandywine." He stared at her. Her heart sank. "Oh God, you do."

"The battle be over."

He was crazy. She was dealing with crazy people. She should be scared. Really scared.

And yet, she felt oddly safe in the company of this man. That made the least sense of all.

"Okay," she said, stalling, "if this is the Battle of Brandywine, what day is it?"

He looked at her strangely. "September the seventeenth."

"And the year?"

"Do you not know the year?"

"Slipped my mind."

"The Year of Our Lord seventeen hundred and seventy-seven."

Again that shiver down her spine, but she pressed on. "How many troops do you British have?"

"A force of no less than eight thousand – more than enough to vanquish the rebel army."

"Did you forget something from history class?"

His eyes narrowed and his jaw hardened in displeasure.

"Like the Americans winning the War of Independence?" Pauline reminded him. They must have used a different textbook for crazy Amish people who liked to pretend they were in the eighteenth century.

"The 'Americans' you speak of can barely provide shoes for the soldiers in their army, let alone win a war."

"True, but don't underestimate the shoeless soldiers of Washington. And while you may have won the Battle of Brandywine with lopsided casualties, General Burgoyne is about to lose the Battle of Saratoga, and that, my friend, brings in the French."

Pauline paused. Why was she having this conversation? His grip on her arm sharpened painfully.

"How do you know this?"

"Ow. Because I aced all my American history classes, okay? Could you let go?"

Instead of releasing her, he brought her closer to him. "You know the casualties of the battle?"

"Well, there are no official records on the American side, but I think it was estimated to be more than a thousand. The British had fewer than six hundred, I think, but you should know that part." The look on his face worried her. "Can I go now?"

"You are to come with me."

"No, I'm not," Pauline insisted, trying to yank her arm from him. "I am going to get help. You, however, go on about your merry little battle here."

When he still wouldn't free her, she kicked him in the shins. His hold loosened enough for her to slip away. She had to get away from here.

Captain Bradford caught her arm in two steps. Pauline tried

to kick him in the shins again, but this time he was ready for her. Her foot connected with nothing and threw her off balance. She fell to the ground, bringing the captain with her. Her knee grazed his inner thigh, and she felt him stiffen on top of her.

"This'll cost you more than twenty bucks," she said, trying not to focus on how delicious his weight felt on top of her. What was the matter with her?

"You are in rather a poor position, madam, to require payment for anything," he returned.

Her cheeks reddened, and she tried to shove him off of her. He grabbed both her wrists and hauled her to her feet. She resisted, but in vain.

"Let me go! Let me go!" Pauline screamed. "Help! Somebody help me!"

"There is only the British army at your disposal, madam," he told her and dragged her back over to his horse and pulled a rope from the saddle. She was being kidnapped!

She stepped closer to him, her body brushing against his, surprising him. Then she brought up her knee and connected with his balls. The captain bent double and let her go. She had to quell the odd yearning to see if he was okay and bolted toward where the Visitor Center was. Or should be. It probably didn't make any sense to go back there since she had already failed to see the building, but maybe she had missed something in the darkness. She climbed up the knoll, huffing and wishing she were in better shape. Behind her she could hear the heavy boots of Captain Bradford. She turned to see how far back he was. Her ankle twisted beneath her.

The ground leaped up to meet her. And for the second time, the world went black.

Chapter Four

They fell to the ground, the captain landing on top of Pauline. She felt her breasts mushed into her by his thick, broad chest. The tips of their noses nearly grazed. As their gazes locked, she knew he was going to kiss her, and her head swam with the excitement and inappropriateness of what would happen. Before discretion got the better of her, his mouth descended toward hers, and she tilted her lips to meet him. The instant their lips met, the flame of desire burst in them both. She struggled now, not to get away from him, but to get closer.

It was not a soft and tender kiss, but searing and demanding, as if he had suppressed his lust – lust that was finally unleashed. Perhaps he had been turned on by her striptease. Good.

The captain pulled his coat off her shoulders and planted his hot mouth upon her neck, her collar, the top of a breast. Pauline arched her back, offering her breasts to his mouth. He ripped open the coat to expose her, then palmed both breasts before he bent his head over them and kissed them in feverish earnest. Her nipples pointed through the satin of her bra. More. She wanted more of him. She could feel his cock hard as a rock against her bare upper thigh and tried to stroke it with her leg. As if sensing her desire, Captain Bradford reached underneath him and unbuttoned his breeches. He pushed aside the slip of material covering her pussy and shoved his cock inside of her.

Yes! Pauline closed her eyes and felt her vagina contract about his cock, caressing the length that filled her so deliciously. It had slid into her wet, waiting slit so easily. They were meant to be together. She moved her hips against him, meeting his thrusts, grinding herself against him. The pleasure built quickly. She was going to come faster than she had ever come before. God, it felt so wonderful....

When Pauline woke from her dream, she felt flushed – and wet. Her breath was uneven. She closed her eyes, wanting to fall back into the dream. She didn't have wet dreams that often, and they had never been this provocative, this delightful. She never thought she could get so turned on by a man with powdered hair and stockings. Was he even real?

Pauline opened her eyes. He was staring down at her with those beautiful eyes. He looked as formally groomed as before but had lost the powder. His dark brown hair was pulled back in an orderly queue, and he was clean shaven.

"Holy shit!"

Pauline scrambled to sit up when she realized she wasn't dreaming. She felt sore all over, and it was no wonder for she had been sleeping on a wooden cot with a pathetic excuse for a pillow. The captain's coat, like her hands and the boots she wore for her striptease, was dusty and covered with dried blood. What was she doing here?

"Would you care for a cup of water?"

She blinked at the captain, trying to untangle the discombobulation she found herself in.

She remembered the striptease. Remembered Crystal not showing up. Running toward the Visitor Center. Her struggle with the captain. The sex... No, the sex was a dream. That hadn't actually happened. She felt heat growing in her cheeks and looked away as if meeting his gaze would reveal her dream to him.

"You best have some," the captain said, handing her a tin cup.

Aware of her thirst now, Pauline took the cup. The water tasted muddy. She noticed the smell of coffee and saw that he had food laid out on the small wooden table where he must have sat while she slept.

"Would you prefer coffee?" he asked.

Pauline nodded. Her head still hurt. He poured her a cup, and she took it from him gratefully. Despite her confusion, she found his voice comforting.

"Ugh!" she exclaimed after taking a sip of the most bitter coffee she had ever tasted. But it tasted better than the water, so she forced herself to take another sip.

"How long have I been out?" she asked him.

"I beg your pardon?"

"How long have I been out? Asleep?"

"It is now approaching ten o'clock in the morning."

That was not a good sign. She had slept through the night here? She glanced down at her body to ascertain if anything might have happened to her during that time, but everything seemed to be in its place.

"You gonna eat that?" Pauline asked, referring to the biscuit on his plate. Perhaps some food would improve her thinking, but the biscuit turned out to be no better than the coffee.

"This tastes worse than cardboard," she commented.

"Worse than what?"

"Cardboard. Dried-up wood," Pauline tried. Why did she find herself having to explain everything she said to this guy?

"We are an army," the captain replied, folding his arms, "and have little time for the baking of fresh biscuits."

Army. Right. He was that crazy Amish dude who thought he was part of the British army.

"Tell me what you know of the battle," the captain said.

His tone had changed and now bore an edge. His gaze was unnerving, but Pauline was determined not to be cowed by it.

"Why don't you tell me first who you are?" she returned.

Her question seemed to surprise him a little, but he answered, "I am Captain Kerry Bradford."

"Is that your real name?"

He knit his brows. "For what purpose would I assume another?"

"Am I being kidnapped?" she asked. She was afraid of the answer, but she had to know what she was dealing with here.

"It was you who came to us, Miss Lipps."

"Yes, but you won't let me leave. Right?"

He hesitated, then repeated his original question. "Tell me what you know of the battle."

"Why won't you let me leave? I don't have any money on me. And my family's not rich, so no use in trying to ask for ransom."

She wondered if Crystal had notified the police that she was missing. That was if Crystal herself was okay....

"You are not being held for ransom, madam."

"Then why won't you let me go?"

Again he hesitated, but before he could answer, a soldier pushed aside the flap and announced, "Captain, Major Hurlberry and General Bradford."

The captain stood at attention as two older gentlemen entered the tent. One was tall and lean with a nose that reminded Pauline of a vulture. The other was a little more portly but had the same kind eyes that the captain possessed. Both were dressed in fancy officer uniforms.

"Captain," said the tall one, "what is this I hear of a naked woman running amok in your company?"

The vulture's eyes lighted upon Pauline and narrowed. "What is this woman doing in your tent, Captain? And why is she wearing your coat?"

The captain placed his hands at his hips. "Because, Major Hurlberry, she would be naked otherwise."

"I believe the women of many an Indian tribe live with scant clothing," General Bradford said.

"I'm not Indian," Pauline offered. "Also, the correct term is Native American."

Major Hurlberry took a step back, frowning in disgust. "She speaks English."

"A form of English," Captain Bradford supplied.

"What is this Indian doing in your tent, Captain?"

"I'm not...," Pauline began but trailed off when the captain gave her a silencing stare.

"She fainted," the captain answered.

"Then why is she not in the care of the women?" Major Hurlberry demanded, one thin eyebrow arched high.

"Because she – Miss Lipps be the name she provided – made reference to the casualties suffered by our armies."

"A rebel spy?"

Pauline opened her mouth, but the captain cut her off.

"I doubt the rebels would employ a woman to spy upon us."

"These rebels are capable of the lowest forms of treachery. What did the rebel spy say?"

"She said that the casualties of Washington's army numbered above a thousand and estimated that to be twice ours."

This time it was General Bradford who raised a brow. "Indeed? That is rather remarkable. We have had some ninety killed and nearly five hundred wounded. Miss Lipps, is it? How did you come by this knowledge?"

"I read about it," Pauline replied and was about to add that the information was posted in the museum at the Visitor Center, but Major Hurlberry interrupted.

"Impossible! Only select officers are privy to the casualty reports."

Captain Bradford ran a thumb along his jaw line. "She also made reference to the French. My company managed to retrieve a number of rebel cannons during the battle. They were French cannons."

"Are you sure?"

"Quite so."

"That is grave news," remarked General Bradford.

Pauline witnessed the exchange, almost awestruck by their performance. It was so real.

"What else did the Injun spy tell you?" Major Hurlberry asked.

"I doubt her to be a spy, Major Hurlberry," Captain Bradford said.

"And why would you think that, Captain?"

"Why would a rebel spy seek out the enemy and proceed to dance in front of its soldiers?"

"I was hired to do a striptease," Pauline reminded him.

"I know not the methods of the rebels," Hurlberry responded, flustered. "Perhaps she was attempting to seduce our soldiers in an attempt to obtain more intelligence."

"I found her attempting to save one of our wounded soldiers."

"A ruse. Why are you questioning me, Captain?"

"Because I think you're wrong."

Major Hurlberry pursed his lips and looked from General Bradford to the captain. "A word with you outside, Captain."

Pauline watched the hard set of the captain's jaw. There was no love lost between the two men, evidently, but the captain followed the major out the tent, leaving her alone with General Bradford.

Sensing a kindred spirit, Pauline decided to take a chance. "Look, you seem like a nice person...."

The man raised his brows.

"Sometimes you can just tell," Pauline explained. "It's like an aura that a person exudes. With that skinny friend of yours, it's a little hard to tell if he's naturally a mean and unfriendly person or if he simply got a bad cup of coffee this morning."

The general cleared his throat. "You are quick to judgment, madam."

"Well, yes and no. Sometimes I get it right, but not always. I guess if I were a good judge of character I would be more successful in my dating life. Instead, I'm rather an abysmal failure. Unless, subconsciously I'm looking for the wrong guy – which is what Crystal believes. It's kind of fascinating how human psychology works, that we could unknowingly yet purposefully be setting ourselves up for failure. I'm blabbering, aren't I? I have a tendency to do that when I'm nervous. I'm not a spy. I'm not even supposed to be part of this game. I just want to go home."

He looked at her with sympathy. "In due time, no doubt.

But we are in the middle of a war and must take all precautions."

"But…"

"My son will see that you come to no harm."

That explained their likeness. Like his son's, the general's tone was reassuring, but nothing short of finding herself back in her little apartment with Crystal would put her at ease.

"So, this battle – it's real for you?" Pauline asked. "You're not pretending?"

"I wish I were, my dear."

He pulled out his pocketwatch. A silver pocketwatch. One she had seen before.

"Did you…did you get that from the museum?" Pauline asked, trying to shake off that strange shiver running along her spine again.

"My dear, this watch has been in the Bradford family for generations," the general answered without hesitation as he opened the face to read the time.

Pauline felt a lump rise in her throat as she remembered the small placard in the museum.

"You're Brigadier General Stephen Bradford…."

"Yes. How did you know?"

"I…" *I read about you.*

But the words never made it out. They regarded each other. Pauline desperately wanted to see that pocketwatch more closely. Seeing her gaze on his pocketwatch, the general put it back in his waistcoat pocket.

"Fear not, Miss Lipps, your situation will be handled swiftly and justly," he told her.

He bowed and took his leave. She watched him exit the tent with a sinking heart. There was one other explanation for all this madness. But her high school physics teacher had said one could only travel forward in time, because the faster one traveled, the slower time became relative to the traveler. Moving *backward* in time was not possible.

Then why did that strange shiver just shoot up her spine again?

* * * *

"Your behavior, Captain, borders on insubordination," Major Hurlberry said. "Do not think that simply because your father is present, you may speak to me in such a manner."

Bradford pressed his mouth into a grim line. "My father had naught to do with what was said."

"You will obtain a confession from that rebel spy. We must know what intelligence she intends to convey to the rebels. You may present a report to me within the hour. I expect nothing short of a successful interrogation. You do come highly regarded, Captain Bradford," Hurlberry sneered. "*And*...I expect that as an officer of His Majesty's Army, you will appear more presentable when next we speak."

Damn old bugger, Bradford thought to himself as he watched the major depart. His hand went to his jaw, which indeed wanted shaving. With Miss Lipps in his tent, he had foregone the services of his valet and the barber this morning. He saw his father emerge from the tent.

"He insists the woman to be a rebel spy," Bradford informed the general.

"She is an uncommon woman, this Miss Lipps," General Bradford replied. "Do you wish for me to have a word with Major Hurlberry?"

"Nay," Bradford replied in a hurry. He did not need for his father to come to his aid. "I am quite able to deal with him."

"Good. You are being considered for the position of major for your recent valor in battle. It would be wise not to cross even the likes of Major Hurlberry."

His father was telling him that here was an opportunity: do not fail. Bradford was aware that the general had achieved the rank of major at five and twenty. Bradford was many years behind.

The general placed a hand on Bradford's shoulder. "I could not speak on your behalf, you understand, given my bias, but the discussion sounded promising, and I trust you will not disappoint. God save the King."

Bradford saluted the general before turning to face the tent. He hesitated, remembering the knee she had delivered to him. A successful interrogation was what Major Hurlberry wanted, but Bradford would wager it would be no easy task. This Miss Lips was unlike anyone he had ever met. He could see in her eyes defiance, mockery, and intelligence. As strange as her words were, she was no fool, nor madwoman.

She was deep in thought when he entered the tent, her legs curled beneath her as she sat on the cot. He had never seen such shapely legs – perhaps because he rarely saw the legs of a woman – nor thought that a pair of boots could look so alluring upon a woman.

"I suggest that you disclose all that you know," he advised her, trying not to look down at her legs.

"You have something specific in mind?" she asked with an arched brow.

"It will fare better with you if you tell the truth," he said in as gentle a manner as he could.

"The truth about what?"

"Are you a rebel spy?"

"Is that what you want me to be?"

She was taunting him. She uncurled her legs and brought them to her sides, spreading her knees. He would have been gazing straight into her cunnie were it not for the flaps of his coat falling between her thighs.

He snapped his gaze back to her face. "This is no frivolous matter, madam."

"It's awfully warm in here," she remarked, unbuttoning the first of the coat buttons.

"Miss Lipps, I beseech you, the sooner you explain yourself, the sooner you may be set free."

It *was* warm in the tent. These summers in the colonies were insufferable.

"Am I being held as a prisoner?" She unbuttoned the rest of the coat, which she then pulled off her shoulders, revealing her black corset. The corset had the odd function of pushing the breasts upward and toward each other.

"Until you have answered my questions satisfactorily, yes," Bradford admitted, feeling constrained by his clothes and the smallness of the tent.

"What if I have some questions of my own?"

"Questions?"

"Yeah, like, have you ever had a lap dance?"

"A dance?"

"Lap dance. I take it you haven't. Let me give you a free preview."

Putting her legs together, she swung off the bed. Bradford was grateful that he was no longer staring at her crotch, but now that she was standing, the coat open and hanging off her shoulders, he could see her bare torso and the strange black loincloth that barely concealed her womanhood. He wished he had his own coat back to cover the growing bulge in his breeches.

"Madam, I have asked you kindly," he said, "but it will go poorly for you if you do not cooperate."

She stepped one high-heeled boot onto his chair. "So now you're resorting to threats?"

He wished she would cast aside his coat. Though he stood a good distance from her, he felt, because she still wore his coat, as if a part of him was touching her, as close to her body as his coat.

"It would be wise of you to cooperate," he insisted.

"Can you guarantee my freedom?"

Bradford hesitated. "It would depend upon your answers."

She straddled the chair. "Then I have a proposition of my own. Why don't you and I find a private little spot in the woods – out of sight, out of earshot?"

He was staring at her crotch again. There were no limits to this woman's lewdness.

Bradford pulled at his neckcloth, his agitation growing and his patience waning.

"What's the matter?" she cooed. "Not man enough? Or do you prefer men over women?"

"Hardly." No one had ever questioned his manhood, but why he felt the need to defend himself to this harlot, he didn't know.

"So let's get out of this stuffy tent and go find someplace private in the trees – away from people like that Major Surly-berry."

Bradford could not help a small smile, but they were

getting nowhere, and Surly-berry had made it clear he expected progress.

"If you cooperate, madam, I promise that I will endeavor my best to see you released unharmed and with due speed," he tried. "If not, His Majesty's Army does not take lightly those who would hinder the efforts of the Crown."

"I'll cooperate," the seductress said, rising from the chair and taking slow steps toward him. "But first I really think some alone time would be nice. After all, you're a man, I'm a woman…"

She was going to try to touch him again. Ignoring the throbbing in his breeches, Bradford made one more attempt at reason. "Madam, do not trifle with me. You will cease this vulgar performance instantly or…"

"Or what, Captain?"

She stood an inch from him. His head felt like it was about to explode, and when she ran her hand toward his inner thigh, he grabbed her hand and wrested her to the cot.

Or my actions are not my own, he thought to himself. He said instead, "Madam, you invite harm upon yourself."

He saw the flicker of anger in her eyes. She pushed against him, but despite her size and strength, he was still larger, heavier, and stronger. He kept her body pinned to the cot.

"Get off of me," she demanded as she struggled to wiggle from underneath him.

"Is this not what you sought?" Bradford returned, palming a breast. "After all, I am a man, you are a woman."

"Not in the tent, asshole," she spat. "Anyone can walk in on us here."

He stared into her eyes. She hadn't really meant to seduce him.

"Of course," he noted. "You wish for us to find a secluded place in the woods, where you can perhaps strike me over the head and make your escape."

The look on her face told him he had guessed her plans. For some reason, it irked him that she had no interest in him beyond hitting him with some instrument.

She responded by renewing her attempts to throw him off, but the thrashing of her body beneath his served only to excite him more. One leg of hers was soundly pinned between his, occasionally pressing against his scrotum – he was careful this time not to allow her knee much freedom; her other leg could do no better than glance off one of his. She had tiny wrists for a woman of her size, and he easily encased both in one hand.

"Tell me what you know of the armies," he said, running his hand down the side of her rib. She gasped. "And how you came by your knowledge."

She glared at him. "Go to hell."

Not the best response. He shoved his free hand down between their bodies and cupped her quim. Her struggles intensified with desperation, but the low moan coming from the back of her throat as he rubbed her through her loincloth indicated a possible surrender.

"Tell me," he reiterated.

The sound she made sounded almost like a whimper. He felt wetness between her legs. He would dare her to question his manhood now. Her struggles lessened, and she looked away from him. He could feel her chest rising and falling underneath his. His breathing felt as strained as hers; the sound of their panting filled the air.

Her eyelashes rested on her cheek. Was that a tear glistening upon them? He released her and stepped away.

49

Words would not come. What could he say? What should he say? He had never felt such a combination of heat and wretchedness. Needing a large dose of air, Bradford backed out of the tent and gave orders for his sergeant to guard the prisoner.

What was wrong with him? He never felt such a desperate need for a drink – or to be submerged in a vat of snow. How could one woman make him lose control? Never had a woman excited him, angered him, and tormented him in such a short amount of time. Perhaps the wanton creature simply played upon the weakness inherent in all men, but as a solider he was no stranger to feminine wiles and seduction. He had certainly been propositioned by more attractive strumpets.

Though this Miss Lipps was not without allure. He found her almond-shaped eyes exotic, and her skin, though dark, was smooth and soft to the touch. Her shoulders were wider and her limbs more muscular than the English women he was accustomed to, but an air of confidence attended her less delicate frame. Her smiles were beautiful. He noticed they always revealed her remarkably white and even teeth.

Shaking his head, Bradford decided to take a solitary walk. From the corner of his eye, he could see Willoughby wanting a word with him, but the lieutenant, seeing the dark cloud on the captain's face, backed away.

Bradford doubted that Major Hurlberry would care if the information sought was obtained by means or threat of rape. The captain knew he would never have harmed Miss Lipps, even if she proved to be a rebel spy, but it alarmed him no small degree that he had been tempted to ravish her. Even now his cock failed to completely settle, and memories of how she smelled – astonishingly fresh and sweet, with a faint aroma of lavender – continued to haunt him.

He would have to take the utmost care with Miss Lipps. Somehow, he had the feeling she would prove more challenging than even the rebel army.

Chapter Five

What was wrong with her? Pauline sat up on the cot and dropped her head in between her hands. Granted, she had struck her head twice. Blacked out twice. And she had never in her life blacked out before. Not even when she had been struck in the head by a line drive during a softball game. But if only the explanation were that easy.

That man – Captain Kerry Bradford – was crazy. Attractive. But crazy. He was a total stranger. So why was she craving him so badly? Was it because she was on the rebound? Was her desire a byproduct of being dumped by Caleb? Did it matter?

The captain's touch had sent jolts throughout her body in a way Caleb's had never done.

Or any of her ex-boyfriends. There had been something forceful yet tender about Captain Bradford's touch. And when he had stepped away from her, she felt as if he had taken the air with him. Her pussy had gone wet for him without hesitation, and it pulsed for him now.

"Aaaargh," Pauline growled to herself.

Maybe it was a combination of things. The rebound effect. That time of month. The biological clock ticking. Maybe it was even a premature hot flash. Whatever it was, she wanted Captain Bradford bad.

She rubbed herself through her thong, but it was no replacement for his hand. Better than nothing. Closing her eyes and leaning her head back, she found the outline of her clit through the material and stroked it, thinking to herself that she must be crazy for even being able to turn herself on, given her predicament. Crystal would have been astonished to know how strongly Pauline had come onto the captain. It wouldn't be the first time she had picked up a guy, but shoving her breasts and crotch at a man was definitely out of character for her.

"Madam..."

Pauline jerked to attention, whipping her hand back and closing her thighs. How long had Captain Bradford been standing there?

"Miss Lipps," he began after an uncomfortable swallow, "I gravely apologize ... I beg your pardon for my ungentlemanly conduct toward you earlier."

She stared at him, not sure she had heard correctly.

"I think it best," he continued, "if I were to entrust your interrogation to another."

Disappointment flooded her. She could tell he had felt something, too. His eyes and his discomfort told her he had not been immune to her advances.

"Wait," she said when he turned to leave. "You can finish what you started."

He looked at her with a funny expression.

"I won't try anything on you," she assured him. "You don't have anything here that I could knock you unconscious with – I already looked. But...it wouldn't be very 'gentlemanly' to, uh , leave me hanging."

Now it was her turn to flush.

"I think it would be unwise to continue in any manner," declared the captain. He turned again to leave.

"I'll tell you what I know," Pauline blurted.

He stopped in his tracks and stared at her.

"I'll tell you what I know," Pauline repeated, despite the warning bells that her more rational side was sending her, "if you ... if you finish what you started – what we started."

"You wish, madam, for me to ravish you in exchange for your information?" he asked, bewildered.

Pauline bit her lower lip. This was probably the most idiotic thing she was doing, but how could she take it back now?

"I wouldn't exactly call it ravishing," she said. "I mean, I'm a woman. I have needs. I assume you have needs, too."

God, did she have to spell it out completely and flat-out tell him she was feeling horny?

He walked up to her. "In exchange, you will answer my questions?"

"Yes."

She could tell he was uncertain about her proposal. What was the matter with this guy? Any other normal heterosexual male would jump at the chance.

"Very well, Miss Lipps," he said at last. "I accept your proposition."

He sat down on the cot next to her. He looked her over, unsure where to start. Rolling her eyes, Pauline grabbed him by his waistcoat and pulled him on top of her. She pushed her lips at his and groaned in satisfaction. The captain did not hesitate after that, returning her kiss with equal vigor and grabbing for her breasts. Pauline felt a surge of triumph along with a surge of intense desire, as if she had not had sex in ages.

The force of his kiss surprised her, and she felt slightly

relieved when he moved his hot, searching mouth to her throat. Except that each kiss of the throat flared the ache she felt in her pussy. His lips felt so delightful, so sinful, so agonizing.

"Well, Miss Lipps?" he said after he had her panting and moaning like never before, "what have you to tell me?"

Pauline groaned. She had not thought that he would actually try to interrogate her in the middle of making out.

"Couldn't this wait?" she asked, trying to reach for his cock. But his groin was pressed too tightly to hers.

"I think not, Miss Lipps."

He tongued the soft spot under her jaw, making her pussy gush with wetness.

"Okay, okay," Pauline relented. She couldn't think straight, but she would try her best.

He pulled down a bra cup and licked her nipple. "Do you admit to being a rebel spy?"

"I'm not a spy."

"Then how did you come by military intelligence?"

"I read all about the battle in the, uh, museum."

He bit her nipple, making her gasp. "Do not jest with me, Miss Lipps, or think you can prevaricate with me."

"But…it's true."

Lifting his hips to allow his hand access, he fondled her through her thong. "The truth, Miss Lipps."

Pauline melted at his touch. She searched her mind for a plausible answer, but it wasn't easy when her pussy felt like it was on fire. "I watched the battle."

"Why?"

"I don't know," she murmured, more focused on the scintillating waves of passion being generated in her loins.

He slowed his motions. "Why?"

"Because I was here," Pauline tried, moving her hips against his hand.

"Were you instructed to observe the battle?"

"No."

"You acted of your own accord?"

"Yes."

He flicked a finger at her clit. "I'm not sure I believe you, Miss Lipps."

"I swear to God I'm telling the truth."

Bradford considered the matter for a moment, then resumed his caresses of her clit. Pauline felt her body lighting up.

"Tell me again of the French," he instructed.

"They have great cuisine."

He pinched her engorged clit between the knuckles of his second and middle fingers.

Pauline moaned. "You must know they're no friends to the British."

"What is the extent of their aid to the rebels?" He pushed aside the thong and slid a finger into her wetness.

"Ohhhh. Lots. After the Battle of Saratoga. Full commitment."

He worked his finger into her cunt while he circled her clitoris with his thumb. "French troops?"

"Yes. And ships."

"Are you a French operative? How do you know this?"

"I just...do."

She was close, so close. She hoped he didn't have too many more questions.

"This Battle of Saratoga you named. When did this

happen?"

"I don't remember. I'll check the history books for you." She held on to his shoulders and gyrated her hips to hasten her climax.

He frowned and pulled his hand away.

"It was sometime in the autumn of 1777."

She was rewarded when he plunged two fingers into her searing pussy. She arched her back into his hand as he thrust more vigorously into her, his palm bumping her clit. The sensations swirling in her groin crested, waving over her body. She shuddered and trembled. He led her down from her high with soft, gentle strokes. When she remembered to take a breath, she felt the greatest of satisfaction.

He must think her a wanton whore, but she had never in her life till now made out with a guy she knew for less than twenty-four hours. At the moment, she didn't care. It felt too wonderful. Already she yearned for more.

Pauline opened her eyes. "Um, I need to pee."

"You need to what?" asked Bradford. His penis was painfully hard, but at the moment he was lost in the lovely flush of her cheeks and the beautiful cries of ecstasy she had emitted when spending. He still lay on top of her with his hand between her legs.

"I need to use the ladies' room."

"For what purpose do you need a room?"

"Pee."

"You desire a coat?"

"No! What the hell are you talking about?" She seemed to search her mind. "Piss. I need to piss."

Bradford scrambled to his feet.

"Let me guess. There's no ladies' room around here?" she

asked wryly as she sat up.

"Assuredly not, madam."

"I guess a bush will have to do."

Nothing had prepared him for a prisoner of war such as this one. He could ask Sergeant Dubose to bring one of the women to assist her. Private McGinnis had a wife with him.

"I kinda need to go *now*," she said.

Bradford let out a breath. "Follow me."

He led her to a private area secluded by trees and bushes.

"There's not poison ivy around here, is there?" she asked him as she eyed the spot with skepticism. "My first encounter with poison ivy, I broke out in hives from head to toe."

"Miss Lipps, this be your only choice," he replied grimly.

With obvious reluctance, she climbed over the foliage. He stood at a respectable distance, looking away, but within earshot should she decide to make an attempt to run.

"Um…I hate to bother you…," she said, "but…you got any toilet paper?"

"Pardon?"

She whispered loudly up at him, "I don't have anything to wipe myself with!"

"Madam, you are unreasonable." What in the King's name would she ask for next?

"Well, it's different for women. We can't just jiggle our parts."

He closed his eyes, then pulled out his handkerchief, one edged with lace and bearing his initials. She took the fine linen from him.

"You can have your handkerchief back," she said when she emerged.

He stared at it with shock.

"Don't worry. I didn't use it," she hastened to add. "It's…it's too lovely to use for such purposes."

She wondered if she had gone too far, offended his sensibilities too much. She felt embarrassed. Pauline San Martin embarrassed. One of the few women to try out for high school mascot, she had to endure any number of degrading and vicious acts as only high school students could dream up. But nothing compared to what she felt now. As if she had shown up at a tea with Miss Manners and violated all the rules.

"I … I'm not usually … I don't usually," Pauline stammered, glancing at him only through the sides of her eyes as they walked back toward the encampment.

Why should it matter this much? It was just a game in which she was playing along. Did it matter what he thought of her? She wished he would say something. But the captain kept his eyes forward, as if he dared not look at her in case he incited something else.

"I'm not usually…this forward," she continued, needing to fill the uncomfortable silence. "I don't have any excuses, either. Not like 'I was drunk' or 'I was high.' Though I do feel a little like I'm in the Twilight Zone. Definitely some strange circumstances here. Not sure how I'd explain it to folks when I get back home. I mean, what would I say? That I got abducted by a group of history fans reenacting the Revolutionary War?"

That stopped him. He looked at her with a peculiar expression. "Miss Lipps…"

"Actually, my name's Pauline. Pauline San Martin. So, uh, maybe we can just start all over? Pretend like we're meeting under normal circumstances?"

Though under normal circumstances, she would not be walking about in underwear, and he would not be dressed like an eighteenth century British army officer.

She put out her hand. "Hi. My name's Pauline. How do you do?"

He stared at her outstretched hand, hesitated, then took it gingerly. She sucked in her breath, aware of the warmth, the gentle yet firm grasp. She felt prickles all over, giddy like a girl about to experience her first kiss.

He bowed over her hand. "Captain Kerry Bradford, your servant, madam."

Damn. He wasn't going to let go of the British army thing. But it didn't matter. At least he had that cute English accent going for him.

"Wow." Pauline swallowed, nervous and pleased that he still held her hand. "You must get all the 'wenches' with that line."

He looked at her with some confusion – his favorite expression.

"So, you wanna go for coffee sometime?" she asked, feeling again like an awkward teenager. "My coffee – not yours. I know this great little coffee house, a quaint and rare mom and pop establishment that hasn't been taken over by a chain yet...."

With her hand in his, he stepped toward her, forcing her back a step as if leading her in dance.

"It's in Kennett Square," Pauline continued, taking another step back. "You'd like it. The British camped in that very spot before their historic march to Brandywine. Although you probably knew that...."

Her back bumped against a tree as his mouth stopped her

words.

Chapter Six

He wanted to put a halt to her chatter. Her sudden timidity had sent him over the edge. She could not entice him, stir his loins as she had, and now play coy. His cock would not tolerate it, and so he pressed his lips forcefully upon hers. Her height gave him easy access to her mouth, which he forced open with his own. Though her body had felt of stronger matter, her mouth was as soft and supple as any of the fair sex. Her lips were full and voluptuous, and her tongue gave way delicately beneath his. She tasted sweeter somehow.

With his body, he pressed her into the tree, wanting her to feel the hard bulge she had created in his breeches. He moved his mouth to her neck, kissing the side of her throat, relishing the moans he elicited from her. His hands rushed to undo the buttons of the coat while he tasted of her. Pulling open the coat, he stared at her bosom. He liked the size of her breasts: neither small nor large. He pulled one from its confines and stared at the rosy areola, ran a thumb across the nipple to make it harden.

She groaned, then mumbled, "So much for starting over."

He reached one hand beneath the coat to touch her crotch. Was the wetness from before or new? Deciding it didn't matter, he pushed aside the black material covering her and slid a finger along her clitoris. She responded by pushing her hips at him and encircling his neck with her hands. He toyed with her clit for a moment, though her loincloth interfered.

"Tear it off," she whispered into his ear.

Glad to be rid of the nuisance, Bradford gripped the flimsy material and ripped it from her. He stared at the small patch of hair his action had revealed. She had trimmed it. Good God, what sort of wanton was he dealing with? But he did not dwell on it, for his own breeches were near bursting. With his other hand, he freed his cock. It pointed right away at what it wanted: her quim.

He slid his cock between her legs and allowed it to glide along the now naked folds of her cunnie.

"Ohhhh," she murmured.

With her wetness lathering his cock, he slid in and out easily between her thighs, which she clenched about him. The feel of her hot, wet flesh was almost enough to make him spend that instant. Forcing himself to pace his thrusting, he concentrated on her breasts, freeing the other orb and rolling both nipples between his thumbs and fingers.

"Faster," she urged, her eyes closed in concentration until she gasped and tremors overtook her body.

He felt her legs weaken, and he wrapped an arm about her waist, holding her up as he thrust between her for his own completion. His climax surged from his bowels and out his cock quicker than he would have liked, but he pulled away from her before any of his seed was lost in her flesh. A little of it sprayed upon her boot, but most of it he directed onto the ground. He propped himself against the tree with an arm after she had slid to the ground.

That he was able to bring pleasure to a woman who most likely was no stranger to carnal pleasure made him feel...powerful. He wanted to do more, make her spend again, hear her delicate cries of ecstasy once more.

She opened an eye and looked up at him. "Are you normally this forward with women you first meet, Captain Bradford?"

Bradford felt himself flush. "Not at all, Miss Lipps – Miss San Martin."

"You're really cute when you blush."

"Cute?"

"Attractive."

He felt his flush deepening. It was most unorthodox for a woman to speak with such bluntness, but he found the half smile she gave him rather charming. His gaze wandered to her groin, which she had not moved to cover.

"Your loincloth…," he began.

"My what? Oh, my thong." She waved a hand dismissively. "I got it at Target for two dollars. I may not be flush with cash at the moment, but I think I can afford another thong."

Her statements always engendered myriad questions for him, but he knew Major Hurlberry awaited his report. He offered her a hand and pulled her to her feet, relieved to see her buttoning the coat. He would have to procure something else for her to wear, as he needed his coat back, though he rather liked the idea of his coat about her now.

"You got anything else to eat?" she asked him as they walked back to the tent.

"We have salted pork."

"Sounds, um, interesting. You know what I'm craving right now? A nice, greasy, artery-clogging Philly cheesesteak."

"I fear salted pork be a far cry from a nice cut of steak."

She looked as if she meant to correct him, but instead said, "Your English accent's really good. Are you actually

English?"

"I was born in India when my father was stationed with the East India Company, but I attended university in England and received my military training in Germany."

"Have you been doing this battle stuff awhile?"

"You mean my service as a soldier in His Majesty's Army?"

"Uh, I guess that's what I mean."

"For eight years."

"Do you like it?"

He stopped. Of all the questions she had asked, this one surprised him the most. "Do I like being a soldier?"

"Yeah."

"I have known no other life. My father has served in His Majesty's Army since he was a young man, as did his father before him."

"Well, that doesn't exactly answer the question. Do you have another job?"

"The job of a soldier is rather consuming."

"Would you have rather done something else?"

He thought for a moment. "No. There have been times, particularly in this war, when I have wished myself back in England with my family. But I have a responsibility to my men and to my country. It is a responsibility I find inspiring. Even as a child, I wanted to be in His Majesty's Army."

Strange. He had never disclosed how he felt about being soldier to anyone – not even his father.

"I've always wanted to be a teacher," she said. "I mean, I would love to be a student the rest of my life, but that doesn't pay. I feel like teaching would be the next best thing because you get to share the fun of learning."

There was a glow upon her face as she spoke that he found very intriguing. "A teacher? Have they female teachers in the colonies?"

"I think most teachers these days are women."

How peculiar. Apparently the customs of the colonists differed more than he would have thought.

He left her at the tent with Sergeant Dubose, ignoring the salacious grin the man gave him, and went to acquire other victuals for Miss San Martin. The attire was more difficult. The women did not carry many spare items, and there were no gowns or petticoats long enough for Miss San Martin's height.

"This is *much* better!" she exclaimed after she had climbed into a white linen shirt from his own wardrobe and a pair of breeches and stockings that he had borrowed from the drummer.

The clothes fit remarkably well, and it was clear she was at ease wearing men's clothing. The breeches molded to her body, and he could not help but notice how well the breeches displayed the shape of her ass. He felt his cock hardening.

"Captain, Major Hurlberry," Sergeant Dubose announced.

"Captain, the hour has passed, and I have yet to receive your report," Hurlberry declared.

"What has the rebel spy told you?"

"I have not ascertained that she is a spy," Bradford replied.

"Did you not obtain a confession from her?"

"Why would she confess to being a spy, particularly if she knows that we hang spies, though I have yet to hear of us hanging a woman for spying?"

He could feel Miss San Martin startle to attention.

"Of course we hang spies!" Hurlberry snapped. "Spying is a most dastardly deed."

"Then for what purpose, assuming Miss San Martin to be a spy, would she confess, lest we grant her leniency?"

"Like letting me go," Miss San Martin piped.

Hurlberry ignored her and put the full force of his frown upon Bradford. "Has she told you nothing, Captain?"

"Nothing that proves her to be a spy."

"What of her privileged knowledge of the casualties?"

"It might have been an educated speculation. She claims to have witnessed the battle."

"Why was she a witness to the battle?"

"She is not the only local to have watched the battle."

"What of her allusion to the French? Perhaps she is a French operative."

Bradford hesitated. That part about Miss San Martin had concerned him as well.

"Captain, I am disappointed," Hurlberry said. "It seems you have accomplished little with the prisoner. I expected better from you. Especially given your pedigree."

Bradford clenched his jaw. Hurlberry, having only achieved the rank of major despite his years, seemed determined to place his wrath upon his subordinates.

"Perhaps instead of feeding the prisoner, you should starve her," Hurlberry suggested, eying the salted pork and cup of coffee before her. "Use whatever means is necessary to obtain her confession. Any means necessary, captain. I shall grant you forty-eight hours and expect a full and complete report. I trust you will not disappoint me again."

The major whirled on his heels and left the tent. Bradford let out an oath. He turned to Miss San Martin, but the look in her eyes had changed. She was more distant, more wary. He swore again, but silently.

"Pardon me, madam," he said and exited the tent.

He thought about involving his father, but the general was not the major's direct superior officer, and Bradford loathed the idea of having to run to his father for help. As much as he respected his father, he had his own name and reputation to forge. He could approach Lord Cornwallis and forever make an enemy of Hurlberry. If Cornwallis were to overrule the major, there would be no end to the wrath of that man. He half-welcomed the major's scorn, but he knew Hurlberry well enough to know that the major would avenge his humiliation not only upon the captain but his men.

There had to be another way. If only he knew the truth behind Miss San Martin. Was she perhaps a spy or involved with the French in some manner? She had mentioned a battle in Saratoga as if it were a certainty, but he had heard no word of such a battle. Could she possibly have received information prior to their own communiqués? Had she and the rebels or the French intercepted a royal messenger? He wished he had asked her these questions earlier, but he had been caught in the raptures, had wanted to bring her to orgasm.

She seemed to have one potential weakness: a libidinous propensity that he had exploited once already. But could he do it again? Did he have a choice? He could not interrogate her in such a manner at length in his tent. Due to her cries the first time, he was like to receive enough smirks from his men to last the duration of the war. There was a cabin on a small farm that they had passed on their way to Brandywine. The cabin looked to have been deserted and the fields untilled. He could proceed with the interrogation there.

Miss San Martin might not know it, but she would be better off telling him the truth. Only then could he position himself in an appropriate manner to both serve the Crown and protect her from the hangman's noose. She might indeed be a spy and deserve a weighty punishment, but he could not sanction hanging a woman. Major Hurlberry, however, would have no qualms. Hurlberry detested the colonists and detested Indians more. Bradford could not entirely fault Hurlberry for his disdain of the latter, for the man had lost his brother to an Algonquin raid during the French and Indian War.

By any means necessary.

Those had been the major's words, and Bradford had no doubt that they meant whatever reasonable torture could be inflicted upon Miss San Martin. And torture was what he would attempt. The torture of pleasure. He only hoped it would work.

For her sake and his.

Chapter Seven

This situation was getting out of control, Pauline felt. They were either the best damn actors she had ever come across or completely crazy or…

No. That last possibility was impossible. She was betting on the crazy. There was too much conviction in how they spoke – both Captain Bradford and Major Hurlberry. The captain had been amazingly consistent. The man would have her believing they were in fact in the eighteenth century.

What if they were crazy *and* capable of murder? Well, she wasn't going to stick around to find out!

"Sergeant!" she called to the sentry on duty.

The man walked into the tent, rifle in hand. If she could wrestle his weapon from him before the captain returned…

"It's awfully hot," she remarked to him, undoing the top button of her shirt. "Have you a fan upon you?"

He knit his hairy brows together. "Soldiers do not carry fans."

"How can you bear the heat wearing all that you do?" She wrapped her hair and piled it on top of her head with hand, craned her neck, and ran her other hand along her collar. "I can hardly stand wearing anything at all."

His mouth dropped open.

"You married, Sergeant?"

"No, ma'am."

"You got any money on you?"

"A shilling."

How much was that worth? Pauline wondered. It would have to do.

"For a shilling, I'll let you feel me up."

"Eh?"

"I'll let you touch my boobs."

He snorted. "A shillin' be a high price to pay for that. I can get a strumpet to suck me cock for a tuppence."

Inwardly she grimaced at the idea of sucking the man's cock, but with his pants down, she would have a better chance of escaping.

"Very well, a tuppence."

His face brightened. Apparently he had stretched the truth about the price and was excited to be receiving what he considered a bargain. "I'll give you a blow job you'll remember for life," Pauline purred. "So why don't we drop them britches of yours…."

The sergeant set aside his rifle and went to unbutton his breeches. Pauline tried not to grimace when he pulled down his pants to reveal his hairy pubes. Instead, she smiled coyly and knelt before him. All she had to do was twist his balls until he doubled over with pain, then grab his rifle. She wasn't sure if it was loaded, but it had a bayonet at the end.

"Have at it," he told her, pointing his semierect penis at her face. "It better be damn good for a tuppence."

"Oh, it'll be worth every penny," she assured him, and leaned in as she reached a hand up toward his scrotum. *You get what you pay for, jerk.*

"*Sergeant Dubose!*"

The man turned around in surprise, knocking her to the ground. Pauline looked up to find Captain Bradford glaring at the both of them.

"Captain Bradford, I … she," Dubose stammered, pulling up his breeches. "A temptress she be."

"I don't care if she bloody paid *you* for the privilege," Captain Bradford said. "You will *not* stray from your duty."

"Aye, Captain," Dubose said, standing at sharp attention.

"Bind her wrists," Captain Bradford ordered before pinning his livid gaze upon her.

Why was he so darn angry at her? Pauline wondered. She could feel his agitation as he went about the tent, grabbing a knapsack and filling it with some of his belongings. Something was going on here.

She hurled herself toward the entrance of the tent, hoping to catch them by surprise and perhaps outrun them. It was a long shot, but she was desperate. Dubose was fast for a man his size, and he seized her painfully by the arm. She brought the heel of her boot down on his foot, and he roared like a bear as he let her go. He leapt at her and pushed her to the ground.

"Sergeant, take care!" she heard Bradford say. "I want her unharmed."

"She be as squirrelly as a hog to be tied," Dubose responded, yanking her arms together and winding a rope about her wrists.

"I'm going to the cops with this," she threatened. "This is aggravated assault on top of kidnapping! The district attorney has a new tough-on-crime policy. Don't be surprised if you get the maximum sentence."

She only hoped her threats would not make them desperate. Maybe they were crazy enough to kill her to avoid kidnapping charges.

"But if you let me go, maybe I won't bother the police

about it," she lied. "If they ask, I'll just tell them it was a game. Part of the Battle of Brandywine reenactment. It was all in fun. But nobody needs to even know."

Captain Bradford turned to Dubose. "Gag her."

A dirty rag was tied around her mouth. Suddenly Pauline was really scared. The captain hadn't made eye contact with her since he came upon her and Dubose. Why was that?

Captain Bradford had finished packing. He ordered Dubose to haul her to her feet and bring her to his horse.

"The provisions you requested are in here, Captain," Lieutenant Willoughby said, indicating a sack tied to the bay and eying the struggling Pauline with worry. She cast him a desperate look, but he turned toward the captain.

"The company is in your charge till my return," Bradford informed him as he mounted the horse and took the leash that had been fixed to Pauline's bindings.

They were drawing a lot of curious looks from the soldiers nearby, and Pauline scanned their faces, hoping one of them would come to her aid. None did.

Pauline screamed into her gag and pulled at the leash as hard as she could. The horse neighed and skittered in discontent.

"Do not force me to tie this about your neck," the captain warned her.

She ceased her thrashing. Her heart was pounding in her ears. This was a different Captain Bradford she was dealing with now.

With a move of his hips, he urged the horse forward, yanking Pauline with them. She walked sullenly behind, her mind racing. She had to make her escape somehow. If she could get on the horse, she could ride it to freedom. Too bad she didn't know a damn thing about horses.

The only time she had ridden one as a child, the poor animal had peed in fright at first, then upon realizing it knew more than the rider, had proceeded to go whichever way it desired, constantly taking her away from the rest of the riders and choosing the steepest slope back to the barn.

Her life had just gone from bad to worse.

* * * *

Hundreds. Pauline couldn't believe it, but they had passed by hundreds of soldiers. Maybe even a thousand. Could there be that many whackos interested in acting out the Revolutionary War?

Another mile and all signs of the army encampment disappeared from view. Pauline hoped they might come across signs of civilization or Route 1. Instead, the terrain became less and less familiar. No road came into sight. This wasn't right.

They proceeded for another mile in silence, with only the rhythmic clopping of the horse's hooves and the jangling of the saddle and gear. Her feet hurt. Her boots were definitely not made for walking. Sensing her weariness, the captain stopped the horse and dismounted.

"Water?" he asked.

Pauline nodded. He pulled down her gag and handed her his canteen.

"Where are we going?" she asked after forcing down the water. It still tasted too earthy for her.

"Per your previous request, a private place."

His response alarmed her. Why did they need a private

place? Would they be alone? If alone, that might be a good thing. It would be easier to take on just one person.

"Get on the horse," he instructed.

"Oh, horses and I don't get along," she said. "I've only been on a horse once in my life, and I think it was trying to throw me off its back and break my neck."

"You would rather walk, Miss San Martin?"

Sighing, Pauline stepped into the stirrup, surprised that the horse did not instantly attempt to flee.

"Wrong foot," the captain noted.

"But if I start with my other foot, how am I going to swing my leg to the other side?"

"For a woman, there is no need." He reconsidered. "But if you have little experience with horses, and this not being a sidesaddle, perhaps it is best that you ride as a man."

Grabbing the pommel, she threw her other leg around the horse's back with a little too much momentum and fell over the other side. The captain rushed over to her.

"I'll walk, thanks," she said as she tried to rub what was going to be nice bruise on her butt.

Captain Bradford helped her to her feet. "Try it once more."

With his assistance, she mounted more successfully this time. Captain Bradford also mounted and settled himself behind her and reached his arms around her for the reins. She felt his thighs brush against her butt when he urged the horse forward. They rode in silence for a mile. She resented his nearness. Resented how it made her body warm with possibilities, then resented that he could still ignite such feelings when she should despise and fear him.

They stopped in front of a log cabin that might have served

once as lodging for the farmhands. After helping Pauline off the horse, Captain Bradford unloaded the supplies and stabled the horse below a wood-shingled awning.

Is this where he meant to murder her? Pauline wondered. Though why bring two sacks of accoutrements if that was all he meant to do?

The cabin had two small dirty windows, but inside it was surprisingly tidy for an abandoned structure. The windows and doors faced east, so there was little light this time of day, but Pauline could make out a fireplace, a table, and a chair in the main room. There appeared to be a second, smaller room with no windows to the side. The floor – well, there wasn't much of a floor that she could tell. Definitely not a place you could kick off your shoes and relax in. A bushel of dried tobacco leaves hung from the ceiling.

"Sit," Captain Bradford ordered, pulling out the chair. He put the canteen of water on the table for her.

That he was offering her water was a good sign, Pauline thought to herself. She sat down and watched as he paced in front of the table. He had his coat back now, and looked even more dashing in his full regimentals. She had always had a thing for men in uniform.

"I have no wish to harm you, Miss San Martin," he said at last, "but your situation is grave. I can assist you best if you disclose all that you know."

She fixed him with her hardest stare. This wasn't a game to her anymore. If they really planned on hanging her as a spy, she wasn't going to simply hand them the confession they desired.

"I've told you all I know," she said.

"I don't believe you."

They stared at each other until Pauline looked away. She was still mad at him for the gag, and she wasn't going to give in. It was the one thing of value that made her useful to them. She was worth more alive than dead. She hoped.

The captain sighed. "Miss San Martin, you present me with little choice but to ..."

She was afraid to ask, but she had to know. "To what?"

He walked over to her and cupped her chin with his hand, lifting her gaze to his. Her pulse pounded. Was he going to beat it out of her? Strangle her?

He lowered his head and pressed his mouth on top of hers, not the hard, urgent kiss against the tree, but a tender, firm caress. Pauline melted in her chair. She closed her eyes, all her senses focused on the feel of his lips as they moved over hers. He took his time, each kiss a deliberate exploration of her upper lip, her bottom lip, the corners. He made love to her mouth in a manner that made her head spin. She had never been kissed so slowly, so thoroughly. With his tongue, he urged her bottom lip down, opening her mouth. And then his kisses deepened, taking the whole of her mouth, his tongue pushing and stroking, his mouth sucking the breath from her.

He pulled away and looked at her. She felt the warmth and moisture of his kiss still upon her and longed for more.

"You can do that again," she said, her circumstances and all thoughts of escaping taking a backseat to the heat he had ignited in her body.

A subtle smile tugged at his lips. Standing behind her, he reached a hand to her shirt and unbuttoned the top three buttons, enough to allow him access to her breasts. Thrusting one hand down the shirt, he slid his hand into the bra and cupped a breast. Pauline groaned to feel his large hand

EM BROWN

covering her. Her nipple hardened immediately against his palm. He pinched the nipple, rolled it between his thumb and forefinger, playing with it until she arched her back, wetness forming between her legs. He cupped both breasts and kneaded the flesh. The ache in her pussy began to build, and she parted her thighs, hoping he might put a hand down there.

He stood back to remove his tricorn and his coat. He drank from the canteen, taking his bloody damn time, while Pauline, flushed and aroused, looked on. If he wasn't going to touch her soon, she was going to have to touch herself. When he finished drinking, he simply stood and stared at her.

Bastard. Well, she wasn't going to be shy about it. The longer she waited, the more she needed and wanted to come. Her hand crept toward her mons.

"Allow me," he said, walking over and unbuttoning her breeches with some difficulty.

"These are not as accommodating as gowns."

His hand slid past the band of her pants, and she raised her hips to provide him better access to her clit and cunt. He skimmed two fingers against her clit, dipped lower to find the moisture accumulated there. His wet, slick fingers glided against her easily. He parted his fingers and forked them on either side of her clit. Pauline pressed herself into the back of the chair. Her pussy still ached to be filled, but his strokes against her clit were so delicious, so wonderful. Her climax was going to come quicker than she thought...

...or not. Bradford withdrew his hand and walked back to the other side of the table. When her breathing had slowed and she realized her climax was fading, he said, "I shall grant you one more chance, Miss San Martin. Have you nothing to tell me?"

"Just that you're a jerk," Pauline said through clenched teeth. Her body felt on fire, and she wanted to come so badly.

"Alas, that is an unfortunate answer, Miss San Martin, but I think, before our time is over, you will have told me everything I wish to know—and more."

Chapter Eight

She was glaring daggers at him, and Bradford did not blame her for it. Heaven help him, he was surely going to hell for what he was about to do. And yet, he felt the animal in him, that raw instinct to mate, was in command. He wanted her submission. If he had had doubts about what he was to inflict on her, they had vanished when he saw her on her knees in front of Dubose. He could never attempt what he was about to do on an innocent virgin, but Pauline San Martin was no virgin. She was a wanton harlot. Which should have dampened his lust. Instead, he found himself desiring her above all others.

He untied the sash across his chest and removed his sword. Apparently losing patience with him, she reached a hand down to stroke herself.

"I think not," he interrupted, raising her arms away from her womanhood with his sword.

"Screw you," she spat and maneuvered her hands under his sword.

Pulling her hands up and behind her head, he secured the rest of the rope to the back of the chair. It made her bosom jut out farther.

"I was going to finish the job because you're not man enough to do it," she said, jerking her arms, but they were securely fastened to the chair.

This time he let her comments slide off without a care. In due time she was going to see just how much of a man he was.

The only question was how long he might last. His loins already felt stretched, and his cock was pressing against the tightness of his breeches. With difficulty, he forced himself to finish unpacking, ignoring her exasperated grunting. Eventually she ceased her struggles and sat silently as he went out to feed his mare, then returned with the oil lamp he had brought.

When he was done, he stood before her again. "Miss San Martin, we have two days of solitude. Two days in which you are advised to disclose all that you know. At the end of the two days, we shall return to the encampment. A hearing of His Majesty's Council will be held and your fate determined."

"You said so yourself to Hurlberry that I have little incentive to cooperate," she said without looking at him, her tone ice cold in the balmy summer evening.

"True. But I have since devised an incentive."

She met his gaze this time with a derisive smirk. "Give it your best shot."

He raised his brows at her challenge. She was either brazen or foolish – or both. Without a word, he knelt down to remove her black leather boots. At first she jumped at his nearness, but then she settled into a passive nonchalance. He rolled her stockings languidly down her calves. She had very smooth skin. Next he undid the buttons below her knees and pulled off her breeches. It seemed she lifted her body slightly to help ease the garment off. The crotch of the breeches was still damp.

Her brown eyes were pinned on his every move. Bradford took a moment to appreciate her nakedness, inhaled the musky scent of her womanhood. Parting her thighs, he pulled her to the edge of the chair and studied the smooth folds that hid her clitoris. He ran his thumb along a labium, as soft as the flesh of a babe, then let the thumb slide in between. The hitch in her breath was audible when his digit struck her clitoris. He circled his thumb on the clitoris, encouraging it to enlarge and appear from its place of hiding.

Miss San Martin now had her eyes closed as if in concentration, her face turned to the side, masked of any emotion. Bradford patiently continued to fondle her until the folds beneath glistened with her body's honey. He bent his head down and licked it. Her fluid tasted faintly salty, and sweet in the most uncommon and unique sense of the word. Her aroma, the taste of her, was making the blood pound in his loins. He spread her nether lips with his thumbs and licked her clitoris with his tongue.

"No!"

The word inadvertently popped out of her mouth, but she stilled herself after that. He licked her again and received no reaction, but on either side of his head, her thighs had tensed. The most vulnerable and treasured part of a woman was at his disposal. Taoist manuals referred to it as the Red Chamber. In Tantra, it was the yoni.

He had occasion as a young man growing up in India to frequent the brothels there. He witnessed once two women coupling, and it had amazed him the amount of pleasure the one woman received from her partner. None of the women he had ever been with had exhibited such throes of delight, and it occurred to him that perhaps the shortcoming lay in him. The madam of the brothel, amused by his curiosity, took an interest in him and had shown him there was an art to the carnal rituals of man and woman. Sometimes she had demonstrated the lessons with her own body, which age had rendered less attractive, but Bradford had been eager to learn. His friends never understood and used to taunt him for spending time with the old lady.

In England, Bradford had been surprised to find the brothels drab in comparison. A few visits to Covent Garden and he was done. He took a mistress – an opera dancer. Their conversations were limited, but she was beautiful and enjoyed his different lovemaking skills. He had written to her once after being shipped to the colonies two years ago, but had not heard from her. He knew she did not know how to read, but he had hoped she could find someone who did read and write.

Miss San Martin seemed to suppress a moan as he continued to torment her engorged bud with his tongue. She was resisting his efforts, he could tell. But though it had been a while, he was no stranger to the patience needed to make a woman spend. He was very tempted to grab his painfully stiff cock, but he wanted to concentrate on her. He slid a finger into her quim and heard a small sound in the back of her throat. He rubbed his thumb on the lower part of her clit while he flicked his tongue on its crown in rapid bursts, then slid a second finger into her quim.

She cried out as her body jerked in every direction. A thigh knocked against the side of his head, but he pushed his fingers deeper inside of her, tongued her more vigorously, until she was too sensitive to be touched and was doing her best to keep her pelvis away from him. Standing up, he wiped his chin with the back of his hand and stared at her, legs splayed, small tremors still rumbling through her body.

"Doesn't mean I'm telling you shit," she murmured with her eyes still closed.

"This is only the beginning, Miss San Martin," he told her.

He walked outside, leaned against a wall, unbuttoned his breeches, and pulled hard and fast at his cock. He spent in a matter of minutes. The Indian madam had taught him much, but the next two days would be a test of endurance, and as he leaned his head back against the wall, he wondered how he would survive it.

* * * *

Damn it, he must think I'm so pathetic, Pauline thought, *and some kind of sex-crazed nympho.*

She looked down at her spread legs; she could feel her juices on the seat of the chair. She felt a little like crying. How had she ended up here? And what was going to become of her? The darkness of the cabin only exacerbated her loneliness and fear.

The creaking of the door indicated Captain Bradford had returned. Pauline immediately looked up and put on her most defiant face. She wasn't going to show him any more weakness if she could help it.

Using a tinderbox, he lit the lamp and set it on the table. Next he started a fire at the fireplace and brought out an iron pot, which he filled with some water. From a rucksack he pulled out an onion, turnips, and carrots. He cut up the carrots and turnips and tossed them into the pot. Then he took up the onion and stared at it.

"If you untie me, I'll cut it for you," Pauline offered. Her arms were getting sore.

He thought for a moment, then walked over and cut her bindings. With relief, she rubbed her wrists, then reached for the knife.

"I'll cut the onion," he said, holding the knife away from her. He went back to examining the vegetable.

"If you're going to use the whole thing, just slice the ends off and cut it in half. You can pull the skin off easily afterward," Pauline explained. The prospect of fresh-cooked vegetables was a feast compared to the dried biscuits and salted pork she had had earlier.

"You have worked in a kitchen before?" he asked after he did as she suggested and tossed the onion into the pot.

"No, I learned from watching my mother."

"Ah, she was a kitchen maid."

"No. She was an elementary school teacher." Pauline bit her lip. When would she get to see her family again?

When he spoke, there was a touch of sympathy in his tone, as if he sensed her sadness.

"And your father? What sort of man was he?"

"A good sort. Sometimes a little harsh on me and my brother when we were growing up. He was a lawyer – not the wealthy kind. He practiced immigration law. We were a solid middleclass family."

"Middle-class?'"

"Yeah, the um, what you'd call bourgeoisie, I guess. What about you? I take it since you don't know how to cut an onion, you must be of the aristocracy?"

Bradford shook his head. "No, but we had servants to do the cooking."

"I wonder what that's like. To have servants."

He raised his brows. "Did you not have any?"

"No. We could barely afford the second car…. I mean, no, we couldn't afford any servants."

She watched as he spooned the cooked vegetables into a

bowl and handed it to her with a piece of bread.

"Well, it's not every day I get a man cooking for me," Pauline said, feeling more at ease and rather enjoying their conversation.

"I have rarely ever had to cook," Captain Bradford admitted.

She took a spoonful of the turnip. Not her favorite vegetable. A little undercooked. But she was hungry.

"Do you have more family in England?" she asked.

"A mother and sister."

"Do you miss them?"

"On occasion. I would sooner be in England at the moment. It is a tragic war we fight with our brothers."

"Then how do you do it? How do you take up arms if you view the Americans as your brothers?"

"Duty," he said as if that were an obvious answer.

Pauline stared into her vegetable stew, then forced the question she was half afraid to ask.

"Are you really going to hang me?"

"I can assist your case if you reveal all that you know."

She stared at him. "I don't believe you. You see, you don't have the Bill of Rights to protect people from being compelled to bear witness against themselves."

"The justice of His Majesty's Army is fair and bears little reproach."

"You're fighting a war you don't believe in, and you expect me to feel confident about that? Besides, I'd hardly call taxation without representation fair."

He responded with a wry grin. "A favorite cry of your rebel leaders."

"You must admit they're eloquent."

"Eloquent? They distort the truth. Compared to what the citizenry of England must pay, the taxes in the colonies are a relief. But your rebel leaders would have you believe that the weight of the world must be borne upon your shoulders."

"Not the world. Just the tyranny of the King."

"Ah, yes, you vilify His Majesty because it suits your purpose."

She pressed her lips in a grim line. She wasn't used to having the Founding Fathers characterized in such a manner. Samuel Adams, Patrick Henry, and Thomas Jefferson. They were honorable men – weren't they? At least that's how the history books portrayed them.

Heroes.

"This is pointless conversation," Pauline declared, pushing away her bowl. "The end result is that we win our independence and go on to become the most influential country in the world."

"Indeed? How is that possible? With Washington's band of squirrel hunters shooting from behind trees like cowards?"

"Well, if you're stupid enough to form a target out in the open with your bright red coats, you've only yourself to blame." Pauline crossed her arms. It was one of her better comebacks, and despite the fact that she wasn't wearing any pants, she felt quite superior for it. Except he seemed amused by her comment, and that ruffled her.

"Besides," she added, "those squirrel hunters are better soldiers than you give them credit for."

"Your rebel soldiers may be good marksmen, but soldiers they are not."

"Well, Baron von Steuben will soon change that."

When the Captain's brows rose, Pauline realized she

should have kept her mouth shut.

"A Prussian?"

Pauline looked down at her lap, trying to find a way to backpedal from her assertion. The easygoing air of their prior conversation was gone, and tension took its place. She searched her mind for a way to escape. The sound of his boots approaching her table made her look up. "There is much you seem to know, Miss San Martin," he said, his gaze pinning her to the chair despite her urgent desire to bolt.

How she desperately wished she could explain! But her true explanation would only serve to make him more suspicious of her, wouldn't it? He might think she was mocking him.

"I … I hear things," Pauline replied with a shrug, but her response sounded lame even to her. "And what else have you heard?"

"I'm just going to put the pants back on," she informed him as she reached for where he had tossed the breeches earlier.

He reached the breeches before her and swept them away. "I think not, Miss San Martin."

Her mouth went dry. Her pussy tingled. She backed away from him, but there was little real estate in the little cabin, and she was soon against a wall. He stepped up to her.

"You will tell me all that you know, Miss San Martin."

"Why? Because you're going to torture me with orgasms?" Pauline let out a nervous laugh. She didn't like this feeling of having her back against the wall – literally and figuratively.

She needed to find the upper hand, wanted to be on offense rather than defense.

Lifting her chin, she looked him in the eye. "Bring it on."

Chapter Nine

The challenge was clear despite her peculiar choice of words. His cock had leaped to attention upon seeing her tilted chin and her defiant gaze. He had given her a taste of what was to come, and her cries of delight had been a sweet reward. His head swam with the possibilities. He looked down at her lips, supple and full, hanging a breath away from his mouth, there for him to claim. The lips parted of their own accord, and Bradford could wait no longer. Dropping his mouth down to hers, he tasted of her, felt the softness of her womanhood.

She returned his kiss. Exhilaration flared in his body, and he pressed her to the wall, covering her with his body, seeking more contact. Her kiss was firm, unlike the lazy kisses of some women whose mouths reminded him of pliant dough that wanted him to do all the kneading. Miss San Martin's kisses indicated she was not submitting. She pushed her tongue into his mouth, making him want to ram his cock into her cunnie something fierce.

Placing his hand at the base of her head, he tilted her face farther that he might have better access to her mouth as well as her throat. Their mouths explored each other hungrily. He nipped her earlobe and her neck while he pushed his hips at her. She responded by grinding her own against him. Her fingers went through his hair and held his head in place as if depriving her of his mouth would deprive her of air. He could feel her desire. He thought he could smell it.

"Tell me more of this Baron von Steuben," he murmured into her neck as he reached his free hand beneath her shirt and grabbed a breast.

"Telling you about him won't aid your cause," she replied in between deep breaths.

He pulled away and began to unbutton her shirt. It had been hard focusing his attention on the vegetables earlier when all he wanted to do was stare at her and think how provocative she looked wearing naught but his shirt.

"Allow me to be the judge of that," he said, peeling the shirt down over her shoulders. One did not always have such easy access to the bosom. Untying a woman's stays took an inordinate amount of time.

She reached behind her back, and the corset came loose. It and the shirt fell to the floor, and now she stood without a stitch of clothing upon her body. She had remarkably little hair on her arms and legs, allowing her skin to gleam. It glowed with health and beauty. Her hips and waist, not as straight and diminutive as English women's, had a proportion sinfully seductive in its own way. Dressed from neck to toe, he became aware of how stifling he felt in his clothes.

As if reading his mind, she began to unbutton his waistcoat, and he allowed it. She gazed up at him with eyes glazed with desire as she tried to undo his cravat. Her fumbling hands suggested that she had never untied a cravat before – unusual circumstances for a harlot of her sort. Bradford pulled at the confining neckcloth while she worked on the buttons of his shirt. Tearing the cravat from him, he picked her up by the hips before she could remove his shirt. He couldn't wait.

Her legs wrapped themselves around his waist. Back

pressed against the wall, her breasts were now at the perfect height. He pushed one up into his mouth and sucked on its nipple. First delicately. Then vigorously. Enough to be a little painful but still pleasurable. Miss San Martin gasped and groaned. He lapped the other nipple with his tongue, playfully bit it, then mouthed as much of the breast as he could, feeling her push her hips at him in response.

"The baron…," he said as he pulled a nipple with his teeth.

"Can't you just fuck me?" she moaned.

He let her fall back to her feet and stepped away.

"The baron," he reiterated.

She ignored him and thrust her fingers at her own quim. He watched her squirm against her own caresses and undid his breeches to pull out his cock, which he stroked in accompaniment. Her face was flushed, her breathing mixed with the most delicious groans as she fondled herself eagerly. He could spend now. With his hand wrapped more securely about his shaft, he had only to pump his cock a little more and his seed would spray upon her body.

But he had a duty to perform. When he felt she was close to spending as well, when she had closed her eyes, her head resting against the wall, her groans more accelerated, he grabbed her wrist and pulled her hand away. This time her groan was filled with frustration. She opened her eyes and glowered at him.

"Miss San Martin. The baron," he reminded her.

"Oh, go screw yourself," she spat.

What the devil did that mean? Bradford wondered. He thrust his hand between her legs and found her immensely wet. He fondled her enough to make her legs quiver.

"Baron von Steuben is just a guy…."

"What sort of guide?"

"No, a guy."

"A what?"

"A man."

Bradford flicked her clit. There was something beyond strange about her language. She circled her arms about his neck.

"I want your cock inside of me this time," she said in a husky voice that made his head spin.

One of her hands slipped down to grasp his cock. Bradford suppressed a groan when she pulled gently at its head. A drop of his own fluid appeared at the tip, smoothing the motions of her fingers as they slid down his shaft. He wanted to push himself farther into her hand and feel himself encased in her flesh. She teased him with a patience that clearly marked her experience, and when her thumb caressed the sensitive spots underneath the head of his cock, he was lost.

Filled with a need to devour her, he cupped the back of her head and crushed her lips to his while he thrust his hips at her hand. He wasn't sure who was seducing whom at the moment, and cared little. He would have her this time.

* * * *

Pauline urged him on by pulling more vigorously at his cock, feeling energized that she was not the only one who was succumbing. She saw him reach into the pocket of his waistcoat and hoped he might have a condom. Though her fairly recent Depo-Provera shot would protect her against pregnancy, she didn't know Bradford well enough to go without a condom. She didn't want to think how crazy she would go if he didn't have a condom.

But what he pulled out was like no condom she had seen before. It had ties at the end.

"Um, does that thing really work?" she asked of the brown, somewhat wrinkled sheath.

"I have one of linen if you prefer," he offered, the tone in his voice indicating he thought her question on the odd side.

Linen didn't sound appealing, and Pauline shook her head. Whatever it was he had, it would have to do. She wanted to feel him inside of her so bad, she thought she would explode if it didn't happen. She watched him roll the sheath down his cock and licked her lips in anticipation. It wasn't easy getting the condom onto his fully erect penis, but at least the thing looked like it fit snugly. Her pussy was dripping.

The little strings at the end of the condom were difficult for the large hands of a man, so Pauline tied them for him. He still had his clothes on, but Pauline couldn't wait to help him off with anything. With the condom securely on, she practically jumped on him. God, she was one crazy bitch in heat.

But the captain whirled her around and bent her over the back of the chair she had been sitting in earlier. His hand snaked around her front, and two fingers began strumming her clit. It felt wonderful, but she wanted more. She wanted his cock.

"What role has this man?" he asked.

Oh no. Not the stupid baron again. She felt the tip of his cock against her pussy lips. Oh yes.

"He teaches the Americans how to use a bayonet and stuff like that," she offered and was rewarded when his cock pushed its head into her pussy. She thought she would melt from the sensation.

"And?"

"And how to march…"

The bulbous head pushed farther into her pussy, and Pauline marveled at how hot his cock felt. It probably had something to do with the condom, which didn't have the cold feel of latex.

"…and other military type stuff."

Bradford pulled out his cock, leaving her pussy empty.

"I don't know all the details," she protested. She wanted to see his face, to see how he could concentrate on anything else. Didn't he want to fuck as much as she did? She was sure he had glimpsed a moment of weakness when she had touched his cock for the first time.

"But he teaches them how to become real soldiers," she continued.

He pushed his cock farther into her. Thank God!

The walls of her cunt grasped greedily at his cock. Just as she had imagined, it felt wonderful to be filled with him. She pushed her butt toward his groin until he was completely buried inside of her. She wasn't taking any chances on this in-then-out game of his. To her satisfaction, he groaned, and she wiggled herself against him, feeling his pubic hair on her ass, and flexed her cunt again on his penis. He shivered.

Grabbing her hips, he pulled himself out and thrust back into her cunt, making her gasp with the force of it. The angle of his cock made it graze her engorged clitoris with every thrust. The flares of pleasure, the forerunners of an orgasm that were as delicious as the climax itself, surged fast and furious. She moved in time to his rhythm, her breasts swinging wildly beneath her. She grasped the chair tightly as the specter of her orgasm –

No! No! No!

Bradford pulled out of her and let go of her hips, though he kept a hand on her back to keep her in place. He was breathing heavily, and through the haze surrounding her, she thought she heard him curse himself.

"I have never heard mention of this baron you speak of," Bradford said through difficult breaths.

"That's because he's not here yet," Pauline said quickly, the words not tumbling out of her fast enough as her pussy grabbed at nothingness. "He arrives later, in February, I think, and instructs the troops at Valley Forge, where Washington makes his winter camp."

Bradford rammed his cock back inside her. She cried in delight. A few pumps and she was able to recapture the wave of her orgasm. She rode the wave long and hard as it reverberated in her body like a note on a tuning fork. He came shortly after her, just before her legs collapsed from underneath her. She had been standing on her toes to provide him better access to her vagina, and the ache in her calves now made itself felt.

He caught her before she fell to the ground, swept her up in his arms, and carried her into the adjoining room, where he had laid down fresh straw for a bed. Still caught up in the blissful afterglow of their coupling, Pauline didn't bother to complain about the coarseness of the straw. He kept his arms about her, so she nestled her head against his chest. She liked the feeling of him. She felt safe with him in a way she had never felt with any other man.

And for the moment forgot that he might have evidence to hang her.

* * * *

Miss San Martin was breathing in that peaceful, even pace suggestive of sleep. That she would curl as she did into his arms, resting her head upon his chest in such a vulnerable manner, wrenched his gut with guilt and made him feel every part the bastard. He had seduced more information from her. Information that only served to incriminate her further.

Her information was troubling, though the fact that the rebel soldiers might actually learn the art and science of warfare did not intimidate him. The piece that unsettled him as soon he was able to reflect upon all that she had said was that she had spoken of *what was to come*, had made reference to this Baron von Steuben in the *future tense*. She had even provided the month – February – in which she thought the baron's training would occur.

Perhaps she had weaved him a tale and no Baron von Steuben existed or would exist. But was it possible that she could concoct such a fib while in the throes of passion? He felt fairly certain her initial mention of the baron had been an accident, but it was possible she was deceptive enough to make him think it an accident.

He looked down and studied her face in the dim room. Her lashes resting on her cheek. Her lips parted slightly. The curvature of her nose. It lacked the high bridge of English women's and reminded him more of the women in India. Somehow he found it difficult to believe that she could be that dishonest. Cunning, yes, but not malicious. She had, in fact, spoken freely of what she knew until Major Hurlberry had appeared.

And even were she a spy for the rebels, how would a

woman be privy to such military intelligence unless she was the wife or mistress of an army officer? The thought ignited a jealousy that surprised him. It was not a feeling he often experienced. Why such sentiment over a strange woman he barely knew? She disconcerted and flustered him, tried his patience, challenged his manhood, defied him, provoked his lesser qualities, made his flesh burn with sin. Her speech.

He returned to analyzing her other attributes to quell his awakening cock. Her manner of speech was as strange as its content. It was unlike any he had heard, and yet she would have him believe that his pattern of speech was the anomaly. And the way she moved and carried herself. Almost masculine. Neither demure like the women of India, nor passive like the gentlewomen of England. Or the colonies, for that matter.

The image of her on the ground with one leg stretched above flashed before him, and his cock stirred to life. He should remove the sheath and clean himself, but he did not want to disturb her slumber. Her arm fell across her bosom, covering the areolas he had enjoyed tasting earlier. No woman had tasted finer. He wanted more of her body. Would she stir if he were to stroke the smoothness of her thigh? His hand itched to touch her. He brushed a tendril of hair from her face.

He should put out the lamp and conserve the oil. Settling her down onto the straw, he grabbed his breeches and went into the other room to clean himself and the sheath. He wondered about Miss San Martin all the while. Where she came from. Who her family was. They would no doubt be aghast at the impropriety of what was happening. Perhaps her father would come to demand his daughter's honor be redeemed through matrimony. Though Bradford doubted Miss

San Martin concerned herself with her honor.

Picking up a blanket, he went to look upon her. She was extraordinary, this Pauline San Martin. It was as if she came from another world, and though he had seen different parts of His Majesty's empire, hers was one more foreign than familiar. He placed the blanket upon her and turned to tend to his bed and the matter of ensuring she attempted no escape while he slept.

"Don't go."

He turned back to find her eyes, bright in the poorly lit room, upon him. He thought she might be angry with him after their coupling, but she would not have asked him to stay if she was.

"Your servant, madam," he said with a slight bow. "Is there aught I can provide you?"

"Are you always this polite to your prisoners?" she asked with a touch of teasing irony.

"You are an unusual prisoner, Miss San Martin."

She sat up, pulling the blanket over her bosom in a rare move of modesty, and looked
about her. "I take it this is all there is for a bed?"

"I would there were better accommodations," he replied, thinking of his own sleep situation and that he probably wouldn't even trouble himself to remove his boots tonight.

"Where are you sleeping?"

"There is what appears to be a former stable next to the structure."

"Outside?"

"To a soldier it is of no consequence. I have spent many a night with the stars as my roof."

"What if it rains?"

Was she worried about him? It pleased him that she might be.

"You might as well sleep in here where the straw is guaranteed to be dry," she reasoned.

He hesitated. She misunderstood his pause and assured him that she would not club him over the head in his sleep.

"It would be gravely improper," he explained.

"You're kidding, right?" she asked with a half smile. "We just fucked each other's brains out, and you're worried that sleeping next to each other will be improper?"

Bradford flushed. In fact, he *had* considered the impropriety of sleeping beneath the same roof, though they had exceeded the bounds of propriety when he took her to this cabin without the benefit of a chaperone. He knew he had already ruined her – though he was sure he was not the first – and was trying to salvage whatever little decorum remained to assuage his guilt.

"Why would you wish for me to stay?" he asked when he was unable to counter her logic.

Her gaze fell for a moment. "Because it's kind of lonely here. You're the only person I know."

It was an entrée to many questions he had, and he could not pass up the opportunity. "You mentioned a friend," he said. "And a personage by the name of Evan."

"Oh yeah. They…I don't know what happened to them," she said, her voice hollow.

He felt a strong desire to wrap his arms about her again, but it would have been an awkward gesture. Instead, he sat down on the floor opposite her. "They're missing?"

"You could say *I'm* missing."

At his curious glance, she explained that she had been

engaged to perform what she termed a "striptease," a performance designed to titillate and excite the prospective bridegroom—the Evan she had spoken of – and his friends.

"They were supposed to be part of the reenactment," she said, "so when I saw your soldiers, I didn't think anything of it."

"The reenactment?"

She faltered. "They, um, they were supposed to pretend to be soldiers and reenact a battle."

"Any battle in particular?"

She shook her head, but her eyes evaded him, indicating a possible mistruth. But Bradford decided not to pursue it.

"And after your performance," he said instead, "what were you to do then?"

"Go home and pay the rent before our landlord kicked us out."

"Your father is not alive, then, or gainfully employed? You spoke of him as an attorney of sorts."

She gave him a funny expression. "He's alive and working, but I'm a little too old to be relying on daddy."

"Has your father ceased to provide for you, then? You are married?"

He held his breath to her response.

"My father helped me through college, but in my world, you're usually on your own after that."

"You attended college?" he asked, thunderstruck. This bordered on the miraculous – or ridiculous.

"Yes, I know I don't look it – or sometimes act it – but I was one of the top students in my school."

She spoke of it with nonchalance, as if it were a common matter for women to attend college. How could this possibly be true? His eyes narrowed. "Where is it you are from?"

"Well, originally I grew up in Coventry, Connecticut – that's where Nathan Hale is from – he's a soldier you Brits hung as a spy...."

He nodded. "A brave man. I remember his words well."

"I regret I have but one life to give to my country," they said in unison.

"Where is it you now live?"

"Someplace far away, I guess."

Again the hollow ring in her voice. Perhaps she was part of the Quaker community. He had heard that women aspired to some semblance of equality with men in that sect, but a college for women was unheard of. Perhaps her definition of college differed from his.

"And your husband?" he inquired, hoping he did not appear too eager for an answer.

"Don't have one, but I'm only twenty-six years old."

Only six and twenty? He didn't tell her at that age she would be considered a near spinster among his peers.

"Hey," she said, looking offended all of a sudden. "If I had a husband, I wouldn't have done what I did with you. I mean, what kind of person do you think I am?"

His color rose. "I...you seemed..."

"You thought just because I was willing to get it on with you that I'm some kind of slut?"

He was at a loss for words. She was genuinely perturbed.

"Look, I don't exactly blame you," she said, "even people in my time – society – might jump to that conclusion. Though it really gets me that men who do the same aren't viewed as sluts. That kind of double-standard shows you how far we are from total equality between the sexes. But I am *not* some skank who just sleeps around with anyone. And in case you're thinking along those lines, I'm *not* a prostitute."

"I fair recall you had propositioned–"

"That was for a lap dance. Twenty dollars for a lap dance. Totally not the same."

"Indeed?"

"Yeah. Why, you want a demonstration?"

Chapter Ten

Before Bradford could respond, Miss San Martin had pulled him to his feet and dragged him back into the main room. She pushed him down into the chair, grabbed her belongings, and disappeared into the other room. When she had emerged, she was wearing his linen shirt, her black corset visible underneath it, and her boots. She flipped her hair, which had the effect of making it fly in a wider halo about her head. He wondered if the eccentric motion was meant to be provocative.

"You can get this one for free," she told him, leaning against the wall with one leg bent under her. She slid her arms above her head, crossing her wrists as if they were pinned to the wall by an imaginary hand, and pushed out her bosom.

Bradford felt his cock push against his breeches. He had held her in that very position earlier. He wished she had not worn her boots, for he very much wanted to see her ankles, but he had to admit the incongruity of her encased calves and exposed thighs had a very erotic effect. Seeing his gaze directed at her legs, she put the bent leg down and ran her hands from her thighs to her ankles, then back up the legs, one hand lingering on the inside of her thigh near her mons.

Good God. The image of her near naked before him, coupled with the visions he had had upon first seeing her, was practically more than he could bear. He wondered if his men could have refrained from simply looking had it not been for their fatigue, although, as their captain, he had never tolerated anything less than gentlemanly behavior. What must his men think of him now, when he was perpetrating what must surely be the most ungentlemanly conduct?

Miss San Martin had left the top buttons of the shirt undone, and she shrugged one shoulder free of the shirt. The sight of her bare shoulder was enough to make him wish he had brought along some whiskey. His cock stretched farther, and he tried to pull his breeches from his crotch to make room. He watched as she walked toward him, exaggerating the roll of her hips. She stood in front of him, legs spread, then crouched so that her eyes were level with his. She unhooked one of the buttons and gave him an ample view of her cleavage. The shirt slid off her other shoulder.

"No touching allowed," she warned when he reached for the shoulder. He rarely saw naked shoulders and found them to be such an alluring part of the body.

She straddled her legs on either side of his and pushed her breasts into his face. Surely she jested? How could one not touch when she all but invited it with her actions? All he had to do was drop his head and his mouth could be on top of one succulent orb. But he could tell she meant to taunt him, and he kept his arms beside him – for the moment.

She turned and straddled him with her back to him, crouched so that her arse was almost upon his lap. The blood pounded in his genitals at her nearness. She unbuttoned the shirt, and it slid farther and farther down her back. Even the curvature of her spine was entrancing to him. The shirt fell onto his thighs, and he was greeted with the cleavage of her buttocks this time. She bent over and grabbed her ankles.

Zounds. He caught a whiff of her womanhood, and it took all his strength to keep his hands from grabbing her arse and crushing it to his groin. She slipped a finger and thumb into the back of her corset and unhooked it. Bradford made a mental note of it. Much better than the ribbons in most corsets, which no woman could undo without the assistance of another. She turned to face him again, tossing the corset to the ground. The nipples of her breasts were hard and pointed at him. How desperately he wanted to plant his mouth upon them.

Grabbing her breasts in her hands, she massaged the freed orbs before him, running a thumb over the nipples, pulling them with her fingers as she moaned under her own caresses. He eyed her fingers, splayed over her flesh, with envy. When she reached out, all his senses leaped to attention, wondering where she might touch, but her hand reached past him to the cravat he had tossed onto the table earlier. She drew the neckcloth over his shoulder and straightened. At first, she simply draped the starched linen around her own neck as she placed her hands on her knees and circled her hips above his lap. Then she slid one end of the neckcloth down her back and looped it between her legs so that it cradled her quim.

Bradford closed his eyes to keep them from popping out of their sockets. *Mon Dieu.* Cursing in English now proved insufficient. If his valet were to discover where his cravat had been, the man would want to burn it. When Bradford opened his eyes, she was pulling on the cravat, making it rub forward and backward along her most private parts. She dropped one end and looped it around his neck. He hoped the performance was coming to an end, for he feared his cock would burst if he failed to drive it into something warm and wet soon.

She cooed, "I think you've got a little too much on you."

She unbuttoned his waistcoat, which he readily shrugged

out of. Next she unbuttoned his shirt and pulled it off his shoulders. She stopped to stare with appreciation at his chest. Bending her head down, she flicked her tongue against one nipple before gently biting it. Moving on to the other nipple, she swirled her tongue against it, then tugged at it with her teeth. The wetness her mouth left on his nipples cooled in the air but warmed his loins.

With a small smile that suggested she knew a little on the art of torture as well, she dipped her hand between his thighs and grazed his scrotum. When she withdrew, he grabbed her arm and pulled her head down to his.

"Hey—" she protested before he captured her mouth with his.

Consumed with an urge to devour her, he had had enough of her "no–touching" rule.

* * * *

Pauline wanted him as naked as she was for a change, but she couldn't do anything in his grasp, and she wasn't entirely sure she wanted to do more than simply succumb to his ardent kiss. His mouth against hers had unleashed all the desire she had held in check while performing her little routine. And just to make sure she wasn't entertaining any other notions, Captain Bradford put his other hand between her legs and stroked her.

"I wasn't done yet," she told him when she pulled away for a breath.

Holding her with one hand, he unbuttoned his breeches with the other and pulled out his cock – in a hurry, Pauline noted with satisfaction. It felt good to know that he wanted her as much as she wanted him.

"Oh, but you are, Miss San Martin," he assured her and, grabbing her by the hips, pulled her down onto his lap.

She yelped when she thought she might end up on top of his cock. As if reading her mind, he reached behind him and grabbed the sheath from the table. She wrapped her hand around his erection. It pulsed once for her. If she knew him better, she would have loved to wrap her mouth around his shaft. She bet she could have coaxed a thing or two out of him the way he had drawn information from her.

Taking the condom from him, she fit it over his penis. The condom was a little wet and cold, probably from being cleaned. She reached her hand below and cupped his balls. Perhaps she should make a few demands of her own now that she held his family jewels in her hand. But before she could decide what to ask for, his hand went to her head and his mouth claimed hers once more, and she was lost in the force of his desire.

Her own ardor flared, and she kissed him back as forcefully, Frenching him like there was no tomorrow. He pushed his tongue deep inside her, and this time she lifted her hips of her own accord and sat her pussy on top of his cock. He moaned as her twat sheathed him and her ass nestled itself against his thighs. She pushed herself up and down his cock with the impatience of a man. God, she wanted to come so badly on his cock.

Holding her hips, he aided her by bucking his hips against her while pushing her down on him, sending his cock so deep she thought it hit her cervix. She held on to his shoulders and rode him hard, loving it when her clitoris smashed against his pelvis. It was amazing how quickly her climax loomed before her. She hoped he wouldn't start asking questions again, and pulled at his cock with all her might to keep him from thinking.

"By Jove, that is wondrous what you do," he said, sucking in his breath.

"Kegel exercises," she informed him.

Her fingers dug into him. She was coming. The blood was concentrating in her genitals, the sensations compressing into a small area, and then, like a dying star collapsing into a black hole, from her clitoris or her pussy or both – she couldn't really tell – the sensations burst throughout her body, making her limbs twitch, her hair stand on end, her toes and fingers curl.

Having worked hard for this orgasm, she laid her head on his shoulder to catch her breath. While she panted, he stroked her hair. His tenderness didn't surprise her. She liked the feel of his hand massaging her neck almost as much as she liked his more sexual touches. His cock throbbed inside of her, making her quiver in delight. Her vagina flexed of its own accord – little aftershocks of an earthquake.

"Mmmm, that was good," she mumbled into his shoulder and craned her neck to suck on his neck. "Don't you think sex is much more fun when we're not talking about Baron von Steuben?"

"What baron?" he responded playfully.

She sat up and looked him in the eyes, feeling like she could stare at him for hours. "You're not like any guy I've ever known."

That could be because she didn't know many guys from the eighteenth century.

"And you, madam, are unlike any woman I have ever

known," he returned.

"Do you know a lot of women?" she asked, glad that she had found a way to sneak that question in.

"I assume my share."

"Women you've been with? Have you had sex with a lot of women? Are you allowed to have sex with women?"

He gripped her chin with his thumb and forefinger and pinned her with his gaze. "Only with wanton harlots."

She grinned mischievously. "And I've only just begun, captain."

He groaned and smothered her with a kiss. She was going to ride him at least once more before the night was over. No doubt about that. She would do it now if he could be ready. She wiggled her hips on top of him and thought she felt his cock move inside of her.

"And I presume you've been with your share of men," he noted, placing his hand upon her hips.

"What constitutes my share?" Pauline evaded.

"Too many to count?"

Pauline thought about the question sincerely as she felt his cock harden. "Well, I didn't lose my virginity until I was eighteen and in college. My dad kept a pretty close eye on me till then – wouldn't even let me stay out past ten o'clock on prom night. That was embarrassing."

"Prom night?"

"Oh, um, it's kind of like a ball – for young people." He nodded, so she continued. "But I guess I was a bit of a free spirit my freshman year in college. Newfound freedom plus repressed adolescence isn't the best combination. I dated a lot of different guys – men. My first sexual encounter was...disappointing. To this day, I don't know why I did it with him. He was a nice guy, but I remember thinking why in the world sex was such a big deal if that's all it was. It wasn't until my second serious boyfriend –"

"Boyfriend?"

"Beau. Well, it wasn't until then that sex started getting better. It was him and a one-night fling with Marissa."

Bradford's eyes clouded over. "Marissa?"

"Yeah, that was another episode in my wild and crazy freshman year. Good thing I settled down my sophomore year or I would never have gotten into graduate school."

As she ran her hand down his pectoral muscle and past a nipple, she felt as if she were reliving her freshman year. She was hornier than a teenager with raging hormones. If she could feel like this before menopause, she was in for some tough times later.

"What is a 'fling' in your language?" Bradford asked after careful deliberation.

"A one-night stand. A brief physical encounter, one that doesn't involve commitment."

"And you had such an encounter with…Marissa?"

It suddenly dawned on her why Bradford spoke with such a funny cadence all of a sudden. She wasn't sure how a man in the eighteenth century would view two women getting it on. In the twenty-first century, there seemed to be two main camps of male response: outraged moralism or hedonistic lechery.

But it was too late now to retract her words, so Pauline plunged ahead. "We were a little drunk. Marissa was a bisexual – meaning she dated men and women – and she was flirting pretty heavily with me at this party. It was the first time a woman had ever hit on me, and it was, well, kind of flattering."

"Continue."

This time she hesitated. She still couldn't decipher his facial expressions. "We were giggling about something, and the next thing I knew, we were kissing."

Bradford pressed his lips into a grim line.

"It wasn't much. She, well, she put her hand up my skirt – we were in kind of a dark corner, and everyone else seemed too drunk to notice us anyway. And that was it. But it felt good – what she did. I think I had my fastest orgasm with her."

Bradford picked her up and set her down on her feet. Damn. She looked at his cock standing at attention. Guess she wasn't going to get to make use of that erection. Despite his sense of propriety, she hadn't pegged him as a conservative. In fact, even though he thought her a prostitute of some kind, he had treated her in a gentlemanly fashion. And that had surprised her. But maybe this was too much to ask of a man in the eighteenth century. It was too much to ask of some men in the twenty-first century.

Standing up, he adjusted his sheath and the ties that bound it to his cock. Then he picked her up and threw her onto the table.

* * * *

It was maddening what she did to him. To his mind. To his body. His cock. He had never encountered such a temptress. Had she told her tale of pleasure with another of her own sex to provoke him? It was beyond what one might even read in the tales of Fanny Hill. Spoken with such lack of reserve, such aplomb. That was what he found most seductive, more so than the image of her with another woman.

Her eyes were wide, but then she smiled when he pushed her knees apart and settled himself between her legs.

"Would you like details?" she teased.

Have mercy. Bradford did not think he could handle details. He pushed her knees toward her head, exposing all of her to him. He could see all parts of her womanhood in a single glance: her mons, her glistening vagina, the puckered hole of her rectum.

"I remember her fingers against my clit felt like the wings of a butterfly fluttering against me," she told him.

He plunged his cock into her. She gasped. It was such a beautiful sound, the gasp of a woman being entered. Her legs came to right angles beside him, and he held on to her thighs to keep her in place as he thrust into her. The feet of the table scraped noisily against the ground.

"Oh, yes," she groaned.

His cock had sunk into the heated embrace of her quim with such ease, as if it belonged there. What did she feel like without the sheath between them? With nothing but her flesh and her wetness against him?

Did she respond to this woman Marissa in the same manner she responded to him? He looked upon her open mouth, her knitted brows, and the tiny beads of perspiration upon her nose as she rutted against him. She had a strong body, and when she pushed herself against him, he wondered that he might not shove his cock into her womb.

Bradford wiped the sweat from his brow, wishing he had taken off his shirt and boots. And yet he felt he could do this for an eternity, if his cock were willing. Many times he had to fight back the desire to spend. His desire, boiling and bubbling in his groin, threatened to shoot up his cock at any moment, but he fully intended for her to spend first and to spend upon his cock.

"Yes, yes, yes!" she cried, quickening her thrusts.

And then her body shook violently, arching off the table. She grasped the edge of the table as if she meant to break it apart beneath her. He slammed himself into her to hasten his own climax. And it came, as glorious as the first, making his legs tremble. He lay upon her, their heaving, sweaty chests pressed together. He wondered if the sheath would survive until the morrow.

Chapter Eleven

They slept in spurts together on the makeshift straw bed. Bradford could tell they were both tired, and yet if her buttocks grazed his thigh during the course of the night, they awakened from the haze of sleep and the embers of passion flared again. She was insatiable. He was insatiable. Reaching his hand around her waist, he cupped her mons and fondled her clitoris until she spent. She turned to face him and wrapped his cock in her hand. Her fingers skimmed along his cock lightly at first, her thumb flicking over the tip . He groaned each time. As the pressure in his loins mounted, she tightened her grasp about him and pulled harder. He covered her hand with his to prevent his seed from shooting out all over the place.

They settled back into sleep, only to awaken once more in the night. This time he fumbled in the darkness for the sheath and slipped it on. He held her in his arms, his cock pressed against her buttocks as he nibbled on the back of her neck. She sighed and arched her arse higher against him. He slid his cock beneath her buttocks and entered her, felt her shiver in his arms. Was it because he had not lain with a woman in a sixmonth that his desire should rage so? He wanted so much of her, had almost considered entering her sans the sheath to know what she felt like, bare skin to bare skin.

He grabbed her breasts when she pushed herself farther onto his cock. This woman was shameless. Like the madam in the Indian brothel. Only much more passionate. Miss San

Martin cried out, and in that instant he came, a more blunted orgasm than before. He felt very little of his seed seep from his cock and wondered if there would be any left, if he would have the stamina to go at it again in the morning.

When he awoke to find the sunlight creeping in from the other room and Miss San Martin's hand upon his cock, there was no doubt, stamina or no, that he would be buried inside of her. He had slept fitfully, spending most of the night reviewing all that she had said. There remained but one day. One day to wrest the entire truth from her, and he felt he had but skimmed the surface of all that she knew.

She rolled his sack in her fingers and found a spot halfway between his scrotum and his anus, igniting sensations that sent quivers through his legs.

"Just checking your perineum," she mumbled, her face buried in his shoulder.

He had wanted to plant a tender kiss upon the top of her head, but what she had done – and proceeded to do in pressing a finger in that same spot – drove him nearly mad. He flipped them over and covered her with his body. She smiled triumphantly. A beautiful and intoxicating smile. The length of him pressed against her mons.

"What manner of temptress or witch are you?" he asked of her.

"One that wants to get it on with you again," she replied. "You game?"

Bradford did not quite understand her words, but he grumbled an "aye" and ground his pelvis against hers. He had not cleaned out the sheath from last night, but it would have to do. His body would not wait a moment longer. He suckled her nipples. Gently, then voraciously. She wound her fingers through his hair and arched her bosom into his mouth. His hand reached between her legs to find her wet.

He speared her cunnie and grabbed a buttock with one hand, relishing the feel of her body beneath his, her flesh filling his hand, the wet heat of her about his cock. It felt new and exotic. As if he were fucking her for the first time. Her cunnie felt different in this position. His cock felt different. It gave him the stamina he needed despite his lack of sleep last night. The aching bliss writ upon her face made him groan with desire. He stared at her, drinking in every expression that flittered across her face, as he thrust low and deep.

"Make me come, make me come," she mumbled, grasping his upper arms.

Wanting to oblige, he doubled his efforts. Her eyes rolled toward the back of her head.

She gasped. She cried. And then she screamed. He thought he heard his horse neigh in surprise. But he continued to thrust until his own completion exploded within, shaking his body and blinding his vision. He landed on top of her chest, heard her breathing hard. Only after a moment, when the sensations in his loins had settled into a simmer, did he realize she had dug her fingernails into his arms.

He had noticed her fingernails shined with health. Unlike the spotty nails of the whores back at camp.

The camp. They would have return there tomorrow. His report was due to Major Hurlberry. What could his report to Hurlberry entail other than the fact that he and Miss San Martin had spent most of their time making the beast with two backs?

* * * *

Propping himself on his arms to ease his weight off her chest, Bradford brushed his lips along her jaw. "How do you know that Washington will make camp at Valley Forge?"

Pauline sighed inwardly. She was enjoying the post-coitus glow, the feel of her body still melded to his. He could be such a spoilsport. And she had so hoped he would be up for round two.

"Can't you think of anything better to talk about?" she demanded. "I've probably already told you too much. If I tell you any more, well, it ...it wouldn't be good."

God, what if she ended up changing history by telling him history? Except if she did, her history would no longer be applicable, replaced by a new one. Was her existence tied to the old history? Would she cease to exist if a new history formed, perhaps one in which the United States never came to be?

"On my honor," he responded, "it will fare better with you if you spoke the truth."

She searched the depths of his eyes, wanting to believe him.

"Does a major outrank a captain?" she inquired.

"Aye."

"Then I have nothing to say to you, because there is nothing you can do."

"I can plead your case."

"Using my own evidence against me? No, thanks. How do I know I can even trust *you*? I hardly know you."

He kissed her along her shoulder. "What does Miss San Martin wish to know of me?"

A number of questions popped into her head, but she ought to keep focused and try to find out more about his character and the honor he had alluded to.

"Well," she said, "you thought I might have been a whore cheating on my husband. What about you? Are you cheating on a wife or girlfriend? Sweetheart?"

"I have neither wife nor betrothed. There was one whom I might have made my mistress, but she has not responded to my letters."

An arrow of jealousy shot through Pauline's heart. Though she didn't want to hear the answer to her next question, she voiced it anyway. "And have there been other women since you arrived in the States?"

"Arrived where?"

"I mean, the colonies."

"I have lain with one other since my arrival."

Bastard. Why was she not surprised? Did she really expect a man could go for long without screwing someone? His hand brushed her thigh, and she tried to focus her thoughts elsewhere.

"Only one broken heart in your wake?" she asked, trying to suppress her jealousy.

He looked at her in surprise. "It was no love match. She was mistress to another, but I gather she had felt rather neglected when she approached me."

"And that's it? You haven't screwed – lain with any other? Like a prostitute – a strumpet?"

Captain Bradford shook his head. "Strumpets are not my preference."

She believed him. Gratified, she teased him. "You made an exception with me?"

He stared at her hard. "I suppose."

She found it hard to swallow. Had he really made an exception with her? She stared into his beautiful eyes until she couldn't hold their intensity. Her gaze wandered to his nose, his cheek, his mouth. She ran a finger along the bottom of his lips, remembering how superb his mouth had felt against hers. He caught her finger in his mouth and sucked. She worked her finger in and out of his mouth, simulating the motion of his cock earlier. The warmth began anew in her loins.

Maybe there was more she could tell him. Innocuous information that couldn't possibly alter history one way or another.

"Why do you wish to know about Valley Forge?" she asked him, running her finger, slick with his saliva, on his lower lip. She wanted his mouth on top of hers.

"I asked not why but how you knew that Washington means to make camp there. It would seem he does not mean to defend the colonial capital if he intends a winter camp."

He ran his hand along the side of her ribs. She shivered. "Well then, maybe it's not Valley Forge."

Her response did not please him, she could tell, so she added, "I overheard."

"Overheard? One does not 'overhear' such matters." He kissed her throat. "Either you possess intimate knowledge or you lie."

"I'm not lying."

Just not telling you something you wouldn't believe anyway.

"Ohhh," she sighed when his mouth went to cover a nipple. What could she say that would convince him she wasn't a spy? Maybe if he believed she was a strumpet? That could work. When he pulled at her nipple, she decided a fast answer would do. "I did a few stripteases for the American army as well."

"Did you seduce an officer of theirs?"

His hand slipped between her legs.

"Maybe," she murmured as her sensitized clit sent ripples through her groin and abdomen.

"Which officer?"

Her brain felt mushy, and no name besides George Washington came to her. That would have been outrageous.

"Alexander Hamilton," she blurted.

Bradford's head came up. "The aide-de-camp to Washington?"

She wanted his mouth clamped on her breast again. "Sure."

His thumb strummed her clit, but more slowly now as he seemed lost in thought.

"Is that how you came to know the casualty figures from the battle?" he inquired.

Pauline nodded. How many more questions was he going to ask? She reached a hand toward his cock. Maybe she could refocus him.

"And did Hamilton persuade you to enter our camp?"

"No. I told you I was hired to do a striptease." It was difficult to access his cock with his body pressed so close to hers.

"When did you last have contact with the rebels?"

Again she shrugged, feeling the exasperation grow. "I don't remember. It was weeks ago. Lafayette wasn't a generous tipper, so I realized I needed more money, I took the striptease gig that landed me in your camp."

"The Marquis de Lafayette? You seduced him as well?"

Hadn't she said Lafayette? Realizing her error, she corrected herself. "I mean Hamilton. Hamilton was a bad tipper."

Bradford pressed his lips in a grim line. He stood up, pulling her with him, and dragged her into the other room.

Never a good liar, she realized she had made a costly mistake.

* * * *

With one hand encircling her wrists, he reached for a cord with his other and bound her wrists together.

"Not again," she pleaded. "I...it was just a slip of the tongue. It happens. Especially when you don't get much sleep."

"Miss San Martin, you have trifled with me long enough," he told her. He threw the end of the rope over a beam that crossed beneath the roof of the cabin and tied her to it. Standing on the balls of her feet, she hung rather like a slab of a meat in a butcher shop.

Bradford couldn't decide what upset him more: that she had lain with officers in the rebel army or that she had lied to him. It did not help to remember that he had heard Lieutenant Colonel Alexander Hamilton was an impressive and handsome man.

She knew he had tied her well, but she fought her bonds anyway. Ignoring the angry look she gave him, he adjusted his breeches and went outside to feed his horse. He had enough of game playing. He wanted the truth in its entirety. She was playing him for some sort of fool.

His back felt a little sore from sleeping on the hard ground, and he wished he could have removed his boots for the night, though, as a soldier, he was accustomed to sleeping with his boots and clothes on. As a young officer, after having been in his first skirmish, he often had bad dreams about not being dressed and ready to take arms during an ambush.

There was a well in the back of the cabin, and he pulled up a bucket of water, which he used to wash his face and shave. He cut himself twice, cursing the absence of the company barber. After brushing his teeth and clubbing his hair, he felt more refreshed. Ready to face Miss San Martin.

Back in the cabin, she had ceased to struggle. He put on his shirt and decided not to worry with the cravat and waistcoat. There were few opportunities as an officer when he did not have to concern himself with his dress. He made coffee and offered her a cup.

"You'll have to untie me first," she pointed out.

"I shall feed you," he replied.

She looked mortified, insulted. "No, thanks."

"Suit yourself."

He sat down and began peeling an apple, trying to avert his gaze from her naked body. The curve of her breasts. The swell of her hips. The smooth plain of her belly. All so different from a man's. He sliced the apple for himself and poured the last of the coffee.

"Okay, okay," she said, relenting after watching him eat and drink.

He judged the meaning from her tone, but her language differed much from his. He held the coffee to her lips, feeling like a parent feeding a child. Having her at his mercy in this manner made him feel in control. At last. For he did not often feel in control with Miss San Martin. He offered the apple, and she nodded.

Surprisingly, watching her take a bite of the apple slice from his hand was warming the blood in his loins. Even watching her chew proved entrancing. An appetite of a different sort surged through him, and he wanted nothing more than to devour her with his mouth. She looked too succulent with her arms stretched overhead and her body bare for the world to see. The blood was coursing to his cock, and he turned away so that she would not see the movement in his breeches. What a fool's plan he had made to think that he could seduce the truth from her.

But there was no retreating now.

He wiped a drop of the apple juice from the corner of her mouth. She jerked away from his touch.

"I can force the truth from you," he told her, running his hand down a breast to her stomach, marveling at how soft and silky her skin felt. "I would prefer not to."

"Then don't," she spat, trying to move away from his hand.

He moved his hand back up to her breast and grazed her nipple with his thumb. The little pink nub began to harden. "You leave me little choice."

"I need to take a piss," she announced with a touch of petulance and desperation.

Bradford stepped back, crossed his arms, and looked at her. "I'll have the truth from you first, Miss San Martin."

Her gaze snapped to him, and the fire in her eyes could have melted wax.

"I will have you answer all that you know of the rebel army, all that you know of ours, how you came upon this knowledge, and why a person like yourself should possess such knowledge. I will have no more of your lies."

She glared at him in return.

He sat down on the chair, stretched out his legs, and crossed his ankles. "I am willing to wait as long as necessary. Are you, Miss San Martin?"

Chapter Twelve

God, how she hated him. How could she have been so attracted to him? She had thought he was a nice guy, had been excited for herself that for the first time she had been extremely attracted to a nice guy, a gentleman. But now he was just being a bully. What did he expect her to tell him? She had already given him more information than anyone should know.

She shouldn't have had that coffee. The desire to urinate made her clench her thighs together, but she was determined not to give in so easily. She could tell him a lot of lies, make him think that she was spilling it all, but she couldn't trust herself with lies. Too hard to keep track of, as she had already discovered.

This was humiliating. Dangling by a rope, completely naked, while he was clothed from neck to toe, needing to be fed by him, not being allowed a simple function like going to the bathroom. What could she tell him that would get him on her side? He was too honorable to turn traitor. There was probably nothing the Americans could offer him that he would want. He probably wouldn't believe her anyway. Could she tell him what he wanted to hear without incriminating herself?

Pauline shook away the questions. She had to get out of here. As far away from Captain Bradford as possible. If it was possible to end up in the eighteenth century, the reverse must be true. It must be. If she could just escape, maybe she could throw herself back down the knoll she had fallen from, black out, and wake up back in the twenty-first century – and hopefully not some other crazy time period.

But she had fallen down that same knoll a second time and had found her surroundings no different.

Glancing at the captain, still sitting with his legs out in front of him – God, those tight breeches outlined his thigh muscles nicely – she thought she saw a glimmer of doubt, almost remorse, in his eyes, but it was fleeting. He straightened and put on an even more stoic expression.

"I'll just piss on the floor right here," she threatened.

"As you will. You are welcome to clean yourself later," he said, calling her bluff.

She could hold it for a long time, Pauline decided. She had held it once when she was a graduate student instructor. She had held it in for the entire lecture with none of her students the wiser. Had even listened to one student afterward complain woefully about the grade he had received on the last midterm.

The silence between them was bugging her. Especially since all he did was stare at her.

Her arms were getting sore.

"I told you a lot already," she informed him.

"I want the whole truth."

You can't handle the truth.

But maybe she should try? No, they would just as likely burn her at the stake for being a witch as hang her for a spy.

She had to escape.

"You would only use my words against me," she said.

"I promise –"

"What good are your promises?" she interrupted, glad to be throwing it back at him. "Maybe if you let me pee first, I'll think better of you."

She had seen two pistols yesterday. And of course there was the sword. If she could get hold of a weapon, then tie his ass to the chair he sat in so smugly, she could make her getaway.

Bradford shook his head. "The truth first."

A childish instinct prompted her to stick out her tongue at him. She shifted her weight from one foot to another. This was worse than wearing five-inch heels.

"Your arms are undoubtedly sore," he observed.

Maybe she would club him on the head, too, just for the hell of it. A little payback for all this. No. If he was tied up to the chair, there were more *interesting* things she could do to him. Give him a little taste of his own medicine. She could unbutton his breeches, pull out that nice, hard cock, play with it a little, step back and touch herself. She had caught the lustful look when she had performed her lap dance yesterday.

"A sixpence for your thoughts."

A flush crept up her face, but she told him the truth. "Just thinking of what I'd do to you once this is all over."

He raised an eyebrow.

Maybe she could seduce him into untying her. She licked her lips to make them glisten and spoke in her best Lauren Bacall voice, low and husky. "I'd pull out that *large, hard* cock of yours."

Men always liked it when women referred to their cocks as big and long.

"Run my hands down on it," she continued. "What I would really like to do is put your hot, throbbing member in my mouth. I bet you taste soooo good."

She saw him shift uncomfortably in the chair and smiled to

herself. She wondered how much she could earn working for one of those 1-900 numbers. Probably not a lot. Even porn stars didn't earn that much, she'd heard.

"Have you had anyone take your cock in their mouth?" she asked. "Your whole cock? We call it deep throating where I come from."

"And where is it you come from, Miss San Martin?" he asked, doing his best to seem nonchalant.

"A place where they teach you to suck cock to drive men crazy."

He frowned, but Pauline saw a twitch in his breeches. Ah, blow jobs. Men always fell for the simplest of things. She should have thought of this earlier. Just do what she had failed to do with Sergeant Dubose. Once she had his cock at her mercy, she could do anything.

"Men just *love* the way my tongue feels on their cock," Pauline said, pouring it on. "They love the wetness. Love it when I lick off all the pre-cum."

She made a licking motion to demonstrate.

"Miss San Martin, we stray from the subject," the captain said, but she saw a muscle along his jaw ripple.

"My favorite part of the cock is the flare of the head," Pauline went on. "I love to tongue the part right underneath it. And suck. Hard. Until my cheeks are sore."

Was that a groan he emitted?

"Untie me and I can show you just what I mean," she urged, the need to urinate pressing more strongly against her bladder now.

His half-lidded eyes opened fully. He stared at her as if his glance would pierce right through her. Standing up, he cupped her chin in his hands and forced her gaze to his.

"You must think me an extraordinary fool, Miss San Martin," he said with deliberation.

His hand slid down around her neck. Then he pulled her head to him and clamped his mouth down upon hers. Pauline tried to twist her head away, but it was pinned between his mouth and his hand. She struggled to push him away, desperate and afraid of how it would affect her if she succumbed, because she knew how he had made her feel before, how lost in his kiss she had become. But Bradford moved his hungry lips over her mouth. Already she could feel her blood begin to simmer. Not good.

Her mouth opened of its own accord, allowing his tongue inside. She wanted to kiss him back. But if she wanted her wits about her, she had to resist. So she allowed him to plunder her mouth without giving any indication of how wonderful it felt. Sensing her lack of response,

Bradford moved his mouth to her neck, nibbling and sucking.

"Please," Pauline gasped, trying a different tactic. "Please just let me pee."

"At your will," he said into her neck.

"Come on," she pleaded. "This is cruel and unusual punishment."

"You have the means to end it."

He cupped her buttock and molded his body to hers. His erection pressed itself against her belly, which only made her want to pee more. She jerked herself away, and ended up spinning around 180 degrees on the ball of her foot. Bradford wrapped his arms around her chest from behind and squeezed her breasts. He pinched her nipples and prompted her nether regions to ache and moisture to form in her cunt.

She wasn't going to give him what he wanted. Not this time. Not like this. She was surprised that she could even feel aroused when she wanted to pee so badly. His hand skimmed past her stomach towards her clitoris. His forefinger found it, and he began to stroke it.

Not good. Not good.

Her mind searched for something to say, for a tactic that would get her out of this situation. Her education that cost her thousands of dollars couldn't produce a damn thing for her to turn to.

Pressing down with his finger, he rolled her clitoris around. Pauline closed her eyes. There was so much pressure, so much sensation in her nether regions. She had to think of something else. Something that would serve as the antiaphrodisiac. Like cartoons. Snoopy. Elmer Fudd. Nothing hot about Elmer Fudd.

Bradford slid the finger into her cunt. She was wet. Nothing she could do about that.

What was it she was supposed to be thinking about?

He took his finger, wet with her cunt juices, and swirled it about her nipple. The coolness of the moisture made her nipple perk up even further. His finger went back down for more. This time he lathered her clit with it before dipping it back into her cunt. His middle finger joined his forefinger. Her head fell back against him as her legs turned to pudding, hanging uncomfortably beneath her. He rubbed her pussy, and every time his fingers slid past the opening of her urethra, she thought her bladder would go.

This was too much. If he didn't let her go, she was going to have an accident. But he only continued to rub her between the legs, her own moisture smoothing the way.

"Please don't," she implored, and she meant it this time.

It seemed he said *forgive me*, but with all the sensations exploding in her lower body distracting her, she couldn't quite tell.

She squeezed every muscle, every fiber against the onslaught of sensation. She tried digging her fingernails into her palms to refocus herself. But Bradford quickened his motions, and despite her resistance – she couldn't remember ever trying to stave off an orgasm – her climax ripped through her body, jerking her in all directions. Squeezing her eyes shut, she tried to hold back even though she had reached the point of no return, worried that if she indulged in her orgasm, she would forget to hold her bladder in. Her pussy throbbed like mad. Wetness poured down her leg, but it wasn't pee.

Behind her, she heard Bradford pull up the chair. He placed it in front of her and pushed her knees onto it. She heard him fumbling with his breeches, then felt the length of his cock gliding along her slick pussy lips. She didn't try to resist this time. This time, she wanted it. Her limbs felt numb, and yet her body was on fire, wired from head to toe. When his cock pushed into her pussy, she almost bit off her tongue. It was as if his cock was stabbing at her bladder, sending the most amazing and overwhelming sensations through her lower body. She gulped for air.

He spread her ass cheeks to allow his cock further into her vagina, then began to piston in and out of her slit. She moaned freely this time, not bothering to hide her reactions.

"Tell me all that you know, Miss San Martin," he said, and slammed his cock into her, his groin slapping against her buttocks, making them quiver.

"You won't believe me if I did," she replied through gritted teeth. Did he know that this was making her want to pee even more?

"It would depend upon what you tell me."

Oh God, she needed to pee so bad. Or come so bad. She wasn't sure which.

"I know a lot. More than you can imagine," she relented. Breathe. She had to breathe or she'd lose control of her organs.

"Indeed?" He slowed his pace, reached a hand around her front and touched her clit.

She almost passed out. They were already in her favorite position: a cock from behind and a hand on her clit. Couple that with her full bladder, and she was on sensory overload. The words tumbled from her mouth, and she wasn't sure if she was even being coherent.

"The future. I know it. I know what happens. Don't ask me how I know it. I just do."

He stopped, and she could have died from relief. And yet she felt incomplete. His tone was tinged with anger and frustration when he spoke. "What manner of fool..."

He slammed his cock into her.

"It's the truth. I swear, I swear, I swear."

Breathe. Breathe. His cock sawed its way in and out of her cunt. This was terrible. Terrible and fantastic. She felt a small trickle escape and clamped down on her bladder as fast as possible.

"I know the British make their winter camp in Philadelphia," she revealed. "You'll be better off than Washington's army. But you're not getting the reinforcements you need...."

The specter of her orgasm loomed. She didn't know what

to beg for. For him to stop? Continue? So she rattled on, "General Howe is weary of the war. He won't last long. I think it's Lord Cornwallis who replaces him...."

He pounded his cock into her. The small cabin filled with the sound of Bradford slapping against her ass, of her screaming even before her climax broke over her like a tidal wave, tumbling through her body, shuddering, shaking, spasming. She came off his penis, and he had to grab her hips to plunge her back onto his cock. She felt as if she were drowning, and jerked against the rope painfully.

One arm about her waist, Bradford reached for his knife and cut loose the rope. Pauline crumbled toward the floor. He swept her up in his arms and took her outside. The world swirled around her, and she couldn't stand upright. He held her up near a tree. If she was going to urinate, she was going to have to do it with his help. She grabbed on to his arms, her legs weak as a newborn filly's. She had spent so much effort trying not to pee, that she couldn't relax enough now to do it. Especially in front of Bradford.

But her bladder felt like it was on fire, so she did her best to concentrate, and finally she heard the stream hitting the ground.

Oh God, this was embarrassing. And what was it she had said? Had she told him too much? Had she sealed her fate?

Chapter Thirteen

Bradford took out his handkerchief and wiped the inside of her thigh where some droplets had hit. Then he swept her back up in his arms and carried her to the cabin. He sat down on the chair with her. She laid her head against his shoulder. He wanted so much to cover her with kisses. That she would put her head upon him, allow herself to go limp in his arms, after all that he had done to her showed him a trust that he failed to deserve.

He stroked her hair. It was a little coarse compared to other women's. But she was beautiful. Especially with her flushed cheeks, her skin glistening with perspiration.

He didn't believe what she had said. How could he? It was too fantastic to believe. And yet…it explained how she knew some of what she did. That the British wished to make camp in Philadelphia was common knowledge. That General Howe had been denied his requests to Parliament for additional soldiers was not unknown. But she had foretold that no reinforcements would ever be coming. Bradford shook his head. That must be conjecture on her part.

The troubling part was what she had said about General Howe. How could she possibly know that this war was wearing him down ? She was not wrong on that count, for his father, a close friend of the commander-in-chief, had made such a reference to his lordship's state. But how could Miss San Martin know it? And then to make such a bold prediction, that Howe would not see the war to its end. He had to find out more.

But for now he only wanted to take care of her and treat her better than he had.

"I can make a porridge for you," he offered.

"You know what I could use?" she murmured into his neck. "A shower."

"A shower of what?"

"Or a bath."

"There is no bath to be had here. Naught but the river."

Her head perked up. "That might do. How about a toothbrush?"

He had only one for himself, but he went to procure some dentifrice for her. She wrinkled her nose at the grainy paste, but she scooped some onto her finger and applied it to her teeth.

"You have beautiful teeth," he could not help saying. That and watching her work her finger in and out of her mouth was too titillating.

Her teeth were amazingly even, and they were whiter than any he had ever seen.

"Thanks," she said. "I had to wear braces twice in my life – had them in my prom pictures and senior photos – but I guess wearing the darn things paid off."

"Braces?"

"Yeah, um, wire braces that were placed on my teeth to hold them straight."

"Affixed to your teeth?"

Miss San Martin nodded. "Two years at a time."

"Astounding."

Bradford tried to envision what these braces could possibly look like. He had never heard of such a thing.

They fed his horse first before heading to the river. The thought of an impending bath seemed to cheer her. She had an admirable spirit, Bradford decided. To be in her difficult situation and yet manage to converse with a smile took a strong constitution. She had a very open smile. Unlike what he was accustomed to, she parted her lips to reveal her teeth. He supposed if most women had teeth as nice as hers, they would wish to present them, too.

"I guess it's been like three days since I took a bath," she mused. "It's probably been more than that for you."

"It did rain a few days ago when we attempted to reprise the battle with General Washington," Bradford replied.

It was a cloudy day but not gray enough to indicate rain. The temperature was warm, and he hoped the waters of the Brandywine were cool. When they reached the banks of the river,

Miss San Martin could hardly wait. She stripped off her clothing and stepped into the water.

He had seen her nude, but in the light of day, and with the background of flora, he viewed her nakedness with fresh eyes. Her body reminded him of a tiger: lithe and ready to spring. She had flesh in the appropriate places for a woman: the belly, the thighs, the arse, and the bosom.

Having rarely seen a woman without a stitch of clothing, he drank in his fill.

Miss San Martin crossed her arms across her breasts. "You're not prudish about my lack of clothing anymore?"

"You have quite successfully dissolved any reserve I had, madam."

She flashed him a smile. "Good."

He groaned to himself and shed his coat. She waded into

the water up to her knees. Her arse was supple, and he wondered how it would feel under his hand once more and what it would sound like if he gave it a playful slap.

He continued to watch her enter the water while he leisurely unbuttoned his linen. The water swirled past her loins, and he found himself envying the river for being able to touch so much of her at once. She dove in, and for a second he wondered if she would try to swim to her escape, but she surfaced only a few meters away.

"This feels great!" she exclaimed. "You comin' in, too?"

How could he resist? Bradford took off his boots and breeches. She grinned as he stripped.

Wanton jade, he thought to himself but was secretly pleased that she liked what she saw.

He strode into the water.

"Hey, there aren't any weird eighteenth-century creatures swimming in this river, are there?" she inquired.

"The creatures about here hail from the seventeenth century."

An odd question deserved an odd answer.

"Ha, ha," she said as she swam about. "Whaddya know? The captain has a funny bone. Did you bring the soap?"

He joined her in the deeper parts of the river. "It be on the banks near the drying cloth."

She swam away from him back toward the shore. The water dripped down her body as she stepped out of the river. The woman was remarkably comfortable in her nudity. She bent down for the soap, providing Bradford a nice view of the underside of her buttocks.

"What's this?" she inquired, picking up a locket with a gold chain.

"A portrait of my mother," he told her.

"Do you mind?" She opened the locket. "She's a very lovely woman. You have her eyes."

Bradford glided through the water. "Many have remarked upon her loveliness – it went to the depths of her soul. Hers was such a tender disposition, I sometimes wonder that she chose to marry my father."

"Really? I like your father. He's a lot like you, you know. Stoic and formal. But you can tell he has a good heart underneath it all."

"You had words with him?"

"Just a few, and while first impressions can be misleading, I believe they can also be very telling."

He studied her, wondering which of the two his first impression of her fell into.

"You know, sometimes you just get a strong feeling about someone," she continued. "Like it's a God-given truth."

Their eyes met across the surface of the water. He felt a strange force drawing him toward her.

"Hand me the soap," he said.

She stepped back into the water gave him the soap. He worked a lather in his hands, then proceeded to scrub her back. He liked how her shoulder blades protruded and provided definition. The plump madam of the Indian brothel barely had shoulder blades, though the woman would go mad when he kissed her there.

He palmed her arse. At last. His hand slid between the buttocks, grazing her rectum. Miss San Martin inhaled sharply. He applied more lather down her legs, under her feet, between the toes. He washed her arms, and from behind her, he rubbed the soap over her chest and down her stomach. The slick feel of her soft skin had his cock extending upward, but he meant to devote all his attention to her. He took the soap and rubbed it between her legs at her mons. Her head fell back and landed against his shoulder.

Her body writhed in delectable fashion against him as the hard but slippery soap glided easily across her labia and along her clitoris. Her breathing came in little pants. He rubbed her harder and faster with the one hand and wrapped his other arm around her. She grabbed the arm and held on to him as her legs quivered.

"Ohhh," she moaned. It sounded like a plea.

The moans came quicker and louder until she cried out and her body shook against his. He ground the soap harder against her until she tried to push his hand away. Then he eased his hand, allowing her to come off her pinnacle. He held on to her, wishing he could have seen her face as she climaxed. He could see now that her brow was still furrowed. Her mouth hung open as her chest heaved. He wanted to make her spend. Again and again.

He had the notion he could do it forever.

* * * *

Pauline soaked up what little sun was present between the clouds as she lay on the riverbank after her bath. If she closed her eyes, she could almost forget that she was in the eighteenth century – save for the man lying next to her. He was a set of contradictions. On the one hand, she had never met anyone so prim and proper. On the other hand, their sex was wilder than any she had had with the baddest of her bad-boy boyfriends. He was gentle and caring in a way none of her boyfriends had been, but he was every bit as fierce with his lust. She liked the combination.

"Do you think that the continuum of time is like a straight line, or is it circular?" Pauline wondered aloud.

Bradford, also lying naked on the grass, glanced toward her. "The continuum of time?"

"If it were circular, but not always concentric – if one timeline accidentally overlapped another – then it might be possible for one to end up in the wrong place in time."

"Is that a question of science or philosophy?"

"My science teacher didn't think travel back in time was possible, only travel forward in time."

"You studied the natural sciences?"

"In high school. I stayed away from the sciences in college, except for an astronomy class I had to take to fulfill my GE requirements. The astronomy was a fun class, though. You learned things like why the sky is blue."

"And what explanation was presented to you?"

"That light is comprised of many different colors. Blue and violet colors have the shortest wavelengths. They get absorbed by the gas molecules in our atmosphere."

Silence.

"A remarkable theory," the captain noted, "but quite plausible."

"The theory of black holes is that the laws of physics cease to exist at the bottom of the black hole," Pauline continued, more interested in pursuing her initial line of thought, "so maybe there are other instances where our understanding of physics doesn't apply. I wish I had studied more physics. It's fascinating stuff."

The captain was staring at her with an odd expression.

"Why is it you think General Howe will not stay till end of this war? Do you have an end in sight?"

Pauline ground her teeth. He knew how to ruin a perfectly nice morning – or afternoon. She was finding it hard to tell time without a working watch or clock around.

"I don't remember saying anything to that effect," Pauline half lied. She couldn't remember exactly what she had said, but she knew whatever it was, she had exposed too much. "Are you sure you heard me correctly?"

She could tell he was looking at her more closely, but she kept her eyes trained on the sky above. A breeze wafted over her body.

"Miss San Martin, your evasiveness and half-truths only serve to support a guilty verdict."

"Maybe if you hadn't threatened to hang me, I would be more forthcoming."

She got up and went to put on her clothes, trying not to look in his direction.

"That was an unfortunate error on our part," Bradford acknowledged. "What would you have revealed if we had not done it?"

"I'm not falling for that one."

By now she was a little irritated. She didn't want this conversation. And she was angry at herself, for how easily she had succumbed to him and told him a lot of things she shouldn't have. What if the course of history was being changed even as they spoke?

She headed back toward the hut while Bradford scrambled to finish dressing. The desire to flee emerged once again. It was best to focus on escaping, even though part of her wanted to remain with him. But Captain Bradford was like forbidden fruit. The longer she stayed with him, the worse it was going to get for her. The prudent thing was to get away as far as possible and as fast as possible. At the first opportunity.

That opportunity came sooner than she expected.

Chapter Fourteen

Lunch was salt fish and porridge with butter. Captain Bradford did not push his questions about General Howe, but he was constantly staring at her, and it was making her extremely uncomfortable. Pauline tried to prattle on about more mundane matters as she sought a way to escape. Perhaps at night, when the captain was asleep, she could make a break for it. She would have to bring the horse with her or he might be able to cover too much ground in his pursuit. She would be on her own, for there was no reason to think a good Samaritan would or could help her out. But she'd figure that part out later.

"So tell me about India," Pauline said as she forced down a bite of the salt fish. She would need the protein, for who knew what she was going to get to eat after she escaped.

"Hot. The summers are far worse than any I have come across," Bradford answered.

"I've never been, but it must be exciting. I love tandoori and naan."

"The spices there are plentiful. I remember my ayah in India made an exceptional curry."

"It must be neat to get to travel the world."

"Neat?"

Pauline never thought she would have to translate her English to another English speaking person. "Exciting. Fun."

Bradford shook his head. "I would hardly describe travel as fun, especially by sea. The vegetables you prefer will not last a fortnight aboard ship. The quarters are cramped, and the stench at the end of the journey is unbearable."

"Right. Forgot that travel here isn't as easy as hopping on a pl—"

"A what?"

Pauline stuffed her mouth with bread and mumbled, "So what's an ayah? Is that the family chef?"

"A governess."

"Ah. How long was she with your family?"

"From the time I was born to the time we left India for England. She was like a second mother."

"My oldest brother was kind of like that. He was four years older. My mom had to work two jobs to put my dad through law school and while he studied for the bar – that's a test you have to take where I come from to practice law. I have to say, looking back, Ricky made a good parent. And lucky for my mother, I'm told, for apparently I wasn't an easy kid."

Bradford grinned. "Indeed?"

"I always wanted to do what my brothers did. I mean, I could throw a spiral just as good as any of them, but they didn't have football for girls, and my brothers' friends didn't like having a girl hanging around them."

"You had no governess, then?"

Pauline shook her head. "Couldn't afford one."

"And yet you were able to receive an education that comprised lessons in physics?"

"Yes, well, where I come from there's something called public education."

At his inquisitive glance, Pauline felt energized by the opportunity to present what would be a progressive notion to someone in the eighteenth century. This part surely couldn't hurt history.

"It's practically a right where I come from," Pauline said proudly and launched into a description of the K-12 public school system that provided education for both boys and girls, white and black.

"Though there are still inequities and challenges," Pauline continued. "Teachers aren't paid nearly enough for what they do. I mean these days, teachers have the role of being both educators and parents. And there's rarely enough funding. We'll spend billions of dollars on war, but nothing in comparison for the future of our children to help teach them how to avoid war in the first place."

"Billions?" Bradford repeated, uncomprehending.

"Oh, um, well, clearly I'm exaggerating. It would be like thousands of dollars for you guys, I guess."

Pauline wished she hadn't said so much, but she was saved from further questions by the sound of someone approaching the cabin. Captain Bradford went out to see who it was. At first, she worried it was a messenger from Major Hurlberry demanding that Bradford bring her back to be tried and hung as a spy. She looked about the room in panic for something to aid in her resistance. Her eyes lighted on Captain Bradford's swords and his pistols. It was now or never.

Quietly, she crept to where the weapons lay and picked up a sword and pistol. The former weighed heavily in her hand. The pistol was familiar enough. There was a trigger. She wasn't sure if it was loaded. Better stick with the sword. It needed both hands anyway because it felt awkward. Not like the plastic lightsabers she played with as a child when dueling with her brothers and an imaginary Darth Vader.

From the conversation outside, she could tell it was just

two locals curious as to why there was smoke coming from the chimney of the cabin. She thought about running outside and seeking their aid, but who knew how they would react to her. They were bidding the captain good-day and taking their leave. If she wanted to escape, this was as good a chance as any. She steeled her nerves and unsheathed the sword from its scabbard. It was a beautiful instrument: its guard, pommel, and shell gilt with gold. A golden tassel wound around the curve of the guard.

The grip was twisted silver, and even in the dim light of the cabin, the blade gleamed.

The door swung open, and she raised the sword.

"I'm sorry," she said. Why in the world was she apologizing?

Captain Bradford stopped on the threshold. "Put down the saber."

Pauline shook her head, wishing her palms weren't so sweaty, making it difficult to hold the sword. "I'm afraid not."

He stepped in the room and closed the door behind him. She wished he hadn't done that. Now she felt trapped.

"Stay where you are!" she exclaimed when he took another step toward her. Her arms were starting to shake now.

"You know not how to wield a saber," he informed her.

Pauline lifted her chin. "How would you know?"

"It is evident by your position."

"It's sharp. That's all I need to know."

"You would run me through with it, then?"

She wished he hadn't asked that. The truth was she wasn't sure she could do anything to hurt him. She certainly couldn't kill him. But he didn't need to know that.

"I would have you sit down on the chair," she directed, her

mind racing to come up with a plan. She hadn't had time to think everything through.

"*Now*," she emphasized when he stood without moving. Oh God, what would she do if he didn't listen? She pointed the sword at his heart, and was relieved when he sat in the chair by the table. She kicked over the rope that he had used on her before.

"Tie your feet to the legs of the chair," she instructed.

"You could hurt yourself with that saber, Miss San Martin."

"Don't patronize me," she replied and jabbed the point of the sword at him. In her nervousness, it went a little farther than she intended and scratched his cheek. She paled as a line of blood surfaced.

Captain Bradford stared at her, and Pauline nearly capitulated, but she was too scared to speak. He took the rope and did as told.

He was so damn calm. Not a good sign. He should be afraid. It seemed almost as if he knew something she didn't.

She fished another rope from the bag of supplies. "Tie your left arm to the back of the chair."

It required him to twist his body awkwardly, but he managed to secure his one side to the ladder-backed chair. Putting down the sword, she tied his free hand in the same manner with his neckcloth. Now he at least couldn't go anywhere. Her body no longer shook.

"I'll take this with me," she said of the sword. "And some water and your horse."

"You would leave me here to starve?"

"I'll let the first person I come across know that you're here."

"A rebel solider, no doubt," he responded drily.

"I'm sorry, but it's either you or me," Pauline explained, the guilt beginning to gnaw at her already. "All's fair in love and war, y'know."

"And be this war or love?"

Why did he ask that? She suddenly felt terrified. And angry. It wasn't fair of him to ask a question like that. Not now, when she felt so vulnerable. Not when the truth was that she had developed feelings for him. Feelings she shouldn't have developed given what she had endured at his hands.

But no more. She had the upper hand now. She surveyed her work. He was bound pretty well to that chair. He was her captive now. And rather hot looking with the rope wound around him.

Finding her voice, she lifted her chin. "Which would you have it be, Captain?"

This time it was he who paused before answering, "Though it be a more excruciating death, I would rather die by love than in war."

Drat. She wasn't sure what sort of answer she was hoping for, but not that one. It spoke to her sentimental side – a side she didn't often have to confront in her romantic relationships. And the frank way those eyes of his looked at her, penetrating and piercing, befuddled her. She was not on solid ground.

"And I would rather not die at all," she said and hastily threw what she thought she needed into a bag. *Just get yourself out of here*, she told herself.

When she was ready, she turned to face him one last time. "I hope you understand. I mean, if you were in my shoes, you'd understand. I...it..."

With a frustrated grunt, she wheeled toward the door.

"Adieu, Miss San Martin."

She stopped. Dropping her bag in exasperation, she whirled around. "Look, you would do exactly what I'm doing if you were in my position. I mean, putting my fate in your hands would be pretty darn foolish, wouldn't it? Granted, the orgasms were great, but they came at a price. It was a form of torture. You might not think it, though I'm sure if I gave you a dose of your own medicine..."

The thought registered in both their minds at the same time. She felt the adrenaline coursing through her. And the desire.

"I could, couldn't I?" she asked rhetorically and smiled.

Just a little payback.

Chapter Fifteen

All of his nerves alert, Bradford watched Miss San Martin's lips curl into a mischievous smile. Dear God, what did the woman intend?

She sauntered over to him, her sway made more seductive by the flare of her hips. He felt his pulse quicken as she stopped in front of him and raked him over with her eyes. She slid a finger gently along his jaw.

"You're a good-looking man, Captain Bradford," she murmured and pressed her finger at his mouth.

His lips opened for her. She swirled her finger along the inside of his cheek, over his tongue, along his teeth.

She pulled the finger away and sucked on it with her own mouth. "You taste good, too."

His cock began to lift its head. Her mouth clamped down on his, and her tongue replicated the earlier exploration of her finger. She kissed him with an aggression that set his blood on fire, molding her mouth to his, pushing her tongue hard against his. When he returned her kiss, she abruptly pulled away, leaving him to curse the bonds that held him to the chair.

With her thumb, she wiped away the small trickle of blood on his cheek. He had been surprised when she had run the sword at him. He would have laid odds that she could not harm him, but the consequences of a wrong bet could have been dire, so he had complied with her command to bind himself to the chair. In truth, a part of him wanted her to escape. Though it pleased him that she had remained.

Straddling his legs and the chair, she slowly unbuttoned his shirt and waistcoat. She pushed aside his shirt and ran her hands over his chest and down his abdomen. But no lower. Her head dropped, and he felt her tongue on his nipple. It hardened for her. She licked the small nub and blew lightly upon it. Then she went to the other nipple and began to suckle it. First gently then more vigorously as if she meant to draw milk from it. He had never felt such force upon his nipple. He swore.

She had just bitten him. Again and again she tugged at his nipple with her teeth. Bradford grunted, his nipples becoming more and more sensitive with the attention. She alternated between nibbling, suckling, licking, and biting till he thought he would go mad. The blood was pounding in the veins of his cock despite the searing pain in his nipples. The sight of her tongue lapping at his chest, the feel of her breath upon his skin, aroused him. He could and would endure much from this woman.

At last she withdrew, and Bradford took in a deep breath of relief. The fire in his nipples would no doubt last into the morning. She pressed her mouth to his throat and suckled. He closed his eyes and groaned. His cock throbbed with the need to mate with her. It was maddening not to be able to touch her, grab her, plunge his tongue into her mouth, push his cock against her cunnie. He tested the knot on his left arm. It was loosening. The knot had taken a lot of effort, but he had not secured it well, and Miss San Martin had failed to notice.

Her mouth was extraordinary, he thought to himself. How marvelous it would be to have those rosy lips upon his cock. Her tongue teased his earlobe and the soft spot behind his ear.

A shiver went through his loins. As she continued to kiss and suckle his neck, running her tongue up and down the swell of his throat, her hand pressed down on his cock. At last. He grunted his approval as she stroked him through his breeches. Then her hand went lower, cupping his scrotum and squeezing.

"Bloody hell," Bradford cursed.

She gave him a devilish smile. "All's fair…"

He fixed her with a hard stare. She would pay for that one.

"I never quite understood the whole S&M thing," she reflected as she kneaded his testes, "but you bring out something naughty in me, Captain Bradford."

He suppressed a roar when she squeezed him so hard he thought one of his testicles would burst from his scrotum.

"You devil woman," he said through clenched teeth.

"Well that'll teach you to mess with me," she declared. "Who do you think you people are? Sexually torturing innocent women?"

A protest rose to his lips. He wanted to tell her he had never in his life tortured anyone. Not even as a young lad when all the other boys wanted to cook lizards alive for no reason but to see another living being squirm. Certainly he had never tortured one of the fair sex, save for one instant when he was seven and his sister four years of age. She had destroyed his entire collection of toy soldiers, and he had hidden her favorite doll from her to teach her a lesson. Only his father had soundly punished him for it and scolded him for being unkind to Lizzie. His mother, better able to see both sides, had worked with Lizzie to repair all the wooden soldiers. And all was forgiven when Lizzie had presented his collection and even offered a few of her dolls to serve in his toy army.

It hurt to think that Miss San Martin saw their time together only as torture, but he could not deny her anger was justified. He had started with but a vague notion of seducing her and had been surprised at how far he had gone. And how much he enjoyed it. Pleasuring her body. Hearing her cries of ecstasy. It was a thrill beyond any he experienced on the battlefields.

"Then take your revenge," he told her and braced himself for the shooting pain that would make him double over were he not tied to the chair. "I am, shall we say, at your disposal."

She frowned. Her eyes seemed a little sad. "No. There are other ways. Perhaps not as painful, but hopefully more aggravating."

She unbuttoned his breeches and pulled out his cock. Bradford held his breath as she skimmed her fingers over the taut skin. Then she fell to her knees between his legs and slid her tongue along his shaft. She took his scrotum in her mouth and gently tugged, then went back to lapping his cock while her thumb circled the top of it, rubbing the clear, honeylike liquid emerging from the tip over the head. Bradford felt his stomach muscles tighten as heat flared through his loins and abdomen.

Sitting back, she pulled his breeches down his thighs and rubbed the sensitive area between his cock and anus. Scintillating sensations radiated in his lower body. Damnation. He was going to spend before he had a chance to remove the ropes. Miss San Martin lapped vigorously at his shaft, fondled his nether regions, moaning and grunting with him until he felt his seed ready to burst forth.

And that was when she stopped. Her cheeks were flushed,

and she stepped back to remove her boots and unbutton her own breeches. Maybe he wouldn't need to loosen his bonds. She was as aroused as he. Perhaps now she would place herself on top of him and allow him to spend in the sweetness of her quim.

But she did no such thing. Instead, she lay across the table, her legs bent and spread so that he was gazing straight into the pink of her womanhood. She began to caress herself.

The little minx, Bradford thought to himself. She had worked him into a frenzy, denied him release, and now teased him by pleasuring herself while he remained bound, unable to touch himself or her, hanging at the precipice without the ability to go over it. He watched in envy as she writhed and twisted to her own ministrations. Her cries filled the air.

The rope around his left arm fell to the ground, and with his free hand, he tugged at the knot on his right, keeping the activity behind his back.

She trembled on top of the table and sighed with satisfaction. She sat up and looked at him through glassy eyes. He waited patiently for her to hop off the table and saunter to him. The smile on her lips indicated she was enjoying her power over him. But it would not be much longer.

"I suppose," she said, "that since you did get me to come all those times, I should return the favor."

"Then it was not all torture for you?" he returned hopefully.

"I guess not," she answered, "but I didn't have a choice in the matter."

"You could choose not to enjoy it."

"Funny thing for a guy – a man – to say. You have even less control to choose or not than a woman. I can prove it, too."

She bent over and brushed her hand on his cock.

"Please do," he told her.

She ran her fingers through his hair and brought his mouth to hers in a long, hard kiss. His entire body tensed, ready to charge. He needed to leap into battle or fuck her hard. Or both, as the case might be.

Pulling his arms free, he grabbed her by the shoulders. Her eyes widened in shock. He bent her over his legs and leaned over her body to untie his feet from the chair. It was no easy task with her struggling beneath him, and just as he untied the rope, she sank her teeth into his leg.

"Aaargh," he grunted. He smacked her across the arse.

She yelped. He stared at the round hump curved beautifully over his lap. He could not resist another blow to the smooth flesh. It began to glow pink from where his hand had struck.

"Now, my dear," he said, "we will have an end to this."

Bringing her up and around the back of the chair, he tied her wrists to the top rung of its back. Then he knocked the chair over. She sprawled over the back and ended on her knees between the back legs of the chair, her rump nicely arched in the air. Her breasts peeked in between the rungs of the chairback. Leaning over her, he reached under her and the chair and pinched a nipple.

"Ow!" she protested.

He tugged it harder, though not nearly as hard as she had done to him. "I will ask it one last time, Miss San Martin, and you will tell me the truth. You do have the choice, *ma cheri*."

"I don't have the choice to make you stop doing what you're doing," she pointed out.

Kneeling behind her, he slid his cock between her legs. It

glided along her cunnie, wiping her juices there. He heard a low rumble from her throat.

"You would prefer I cease?" he inquired.

"Cease asking questions, yes."

He moved his hips, rubbing his cock against her. "And this?"

She mumbled incoherently. She was fighting. Fighting her body's natural responses to him.

He pulled away and spanked her right butt cheek, feeling as infuriated as she. How dare she raise his own sword against him? Want to leave him? He reached to stroke her clitoris. She jerked at his touch, but she was wetter than before. He continued to molest her most private parts, inserting a finger into her quim, while he pumped his cock with his other hand. She would receive it hard and deep from him.

"Tell me, Miss San Martin," he whispered. "Tell me to stop. Tell me what you know and how you know it."

She shook her head, but he could tell her body was winning, for her hips rocked in concert with his caresses.

"Tell me," he said again as he reached into his waistcoat pocket for the sheath. He danced his fingers lightly on her clitoris.

"Don't stop," she murmured.

"Your pardon?"

"Don't stop," she said. "I want you inside me."

Bradford could no longer hold back upon hearing those words. His cock encased, he shoved it at her quim, wondering for a second what it would have been like to enter her anus. But when the walls of her cunnie pressed down on him, and that sublime hunger flamed in his loins, he had but one thing on his mind. As he intended, he thrust hard and deep into her.

She cried out – from pain or pleasure, he knew not, but he could not stop himself. Reaching around her, he pulled at her right nipple as he pounded her into the chair.

"Harder," she urged.

His mind wheeled. And here he had thought he was showing her who was the dominant one.

"Is that all you got?" she hissed.

Clenching his jaw, he smacked her rump, grabbed the legs of the chair and pulled it and her body to him as he simultaneously pushed his hips forward, plunging his cock into her depths. She screamed in what was both pain and delight. He shoved furiously into her, winding one hand into her hair. It was the animal in him, pure and unadulterated, that was in command now.

Her cries grew louder, and her panting accelerated. He felt perspiration pouring down his face, but he would have her spend on his cock and by his cock only. And spend she did in a violent eruption of tremors, her body spasming in rapture beneath him. The effect as heady as the victory of battle. He had been holding back his own eruption for so long, he had to thrust a few more times before he spent in a blinding fury. His limbs shook as if they meant to rattle his bones to pieces.

He managed to untie her hands and pulled her on top of him as he lay on the floor. Damn this woman. How could she make him feel so powerless that he needed to prove otherwise through brute force? Was he a lesser man for it? The very foundation of who he was faltered in her presence. No one had ever had such an effect on him. It was both rousing and frightening. He wrapped his arms around her, needing to hold her close.

Chapter Sixteen

They spent the rest of the night making love in between a few hours of sleep. Bradford had no fear that she would attempt to escape again, although he by nature slept lightly and would have woken if she stirred.

"You know the problem with the truth you want?" she asked him as she lay with her breasts upon his chest after she had ridden atop him, bucking against him as if urging a horse to gallop.

"You wouldn't believe me," she finished. "I still hardly believe it myself. I don't know how it happened, and I don't know if I'll ever get back...."

Her words caught in her throat. She looked away and mumbled, "I don't know if I'll ever get to see my family again."

In the growing light of dawn, he could see tears glimmering in her eyes. He held her close as she took a ragged breath, trying to contain what he sensed to be fear and sadness. He wanted to assure her she would, that he would help her. He wanted to promise her the world.

She took a deep breath. "I know a lot of what happens in the future. I just don't think it would be wise to tell you everything."

Of course he wanted her to elucidate, but he asked no more questions. It mattered not, for whatever she said would be no further proof that she was or was not a spy or operative. He was convinced, as had been his instinct all along, that she posed no threat to His Majesty's Army.

"So are you going to hang me or burn me as a witch?" she murmured, still resting her head upon him, her eyes closed.

He wanted nothing more than to wrap his arms about her and protect her. From everything. Past, present, and future. The strength of his emotions surprised him. He had felt this way only once before. He had been in love with a flaxen-haired beauty, had courted her, and thought she favored him. But she – or her family – had greater aspirations than matrimony to a military officer. She married a wealthy baronet.

"Pauline...," he said into her hair, the name slipping inadvertently from his lips.

"Miss San Martin is fine," she muttered. "I'm not crazy about my name."

That she could speak so lightly after all that had happened, all that stood in the balance, spoke volumes to him of her fortitude.

He placed a forefinger under her chin and lifted her gaze to his. Her eyes fluttered open.

"Nothing will happen to you," he assured her. "I'm setting you free."

She sat up. "You're what?"

"You are free to go, Miss San Martin. I will hold you captive no longer." He rose to his feet.

She blinked, failing to comprehend.

"If you are in need of money, I have two crowns." He helped her to her feet and went to get his purse, pulling out the coins for her. "As you have no other attire, you will have to take my shirt and the breeches you have worn."

"For real? You're letting me go? What about the spy

thing?"

He let out a breath. "Are you one?"

"No. I've said before. Of course not. I…"

She was on the verge of telling him something, but no further words emerged.

"You will need more victuals than what we have, but you can have what is left,"

Bradford noted as he collected her garments and handed them to her.

"Thank you," she said and proceeded to put on her corset and pull up the breeches.

He glanced at her body for the last time, tempted to ask her to dance for him in the manner she had performed before the men of his company. But he remained silent as he put food and a canteen of water in a sack for her.

"What about your report to Major Hurlberry?" she asked as she buttoned her shirt. His shirt.

She was concerned for him. The fact warmed his soul.

"It is of no consequence," he told her. Hurlberry would be furious, but there was a limit to what the major could do, and for once, Bradford was not ungrateful for his father's influence.

"I can saddle my horse and take you in whatever direction you wish ."

"No, you couldn't." She was ready. "I'll be fine."

"You have no chaperone and will venture out alone?"

"I'm old enough to take care of myself, but I appreciate your concern."

He went to retrieve his pistols. "Load the powder first, then the bullet. Cock the pistol here, and then you may fire."

"Wow, I guess my aim better be good the first time."

"I should accompany you."

"That really won't be necessary."

They both stared. Both hesitated.

"Then we have but to say adieu," he said. "For my part, I must add that I pray you will forgive the trespass and the…"

"Don't. I understand that you're in the middle of a war. I didn't get … it didn't sink in at first."

"Nonetheless, war is no excuse."

"Well, there are worse things than torture by orgasm," she said with a grin. "Is that a tactic you attempt with all your prisoners?"

He colored. "Miss San Martin…"

"I'm just teasin' ya. Although, if we ever find ourselves in the same situation, you are going to get it in spades, Captain."

It was his turn to smile. He took her by the hand and bowed over it. "I sincerely hope that to be the case, madam."

He pressed his lips to her hand. When he met her gaze, she looked as if she were ready to cry.

"Good luck with everything, then," she said and headed out the door. Abruptly she turned around, and Bradford felt a surge of hope that she found it as difficult to part from him as he did from her.

"Make sure your father knows you love him," she said and hurried out the door and out of his life.

He watched her depart with a heavy heart. He wished he could have done differently by her, done right by her honor. Despite her eccentricities, her brashness and unrefined manners, she was a fine woman. He had spent a short but intense period with her, but he had never had cause to question his judgment of a person's character.

He would never meet the likes of her again.

* * * *

"*You let the spy escape?*"

Bradford had never seen the major this livid. It did not become the man, for the major had always been exceptionally pale, and even the summer sun of the North American continent could not seem to bronze him.

"I let her go," Bradford clarified as he stood before the writing table where the major sat.

"Surely you jest," Hurlberry sneered.

The man knew damn well that Bradford was not the sort of man to jest with a superior officer, so he let the comment go unanswered.

"Why would you disobey a direct order, *Captain*?"

The major need not have emphasized the last word, for Bradford was keenly aware of his position relative to that of Hurlberry.

"I deemed her of no harm to this army or our efforts."

"That was not for you to determine, Captain. I gave specific orders for you to obtain a confession from her."

"There was naught to confess."

Hurlberry narrowed his eyes at Bradford. "Then how do you explain the intelligence she relayed?"

Miss San Martin's words reverberated in his head, but he could not repeat them to Hurlberry, especially when he found it difficult to believe himself. She would need to possess sorcery of some kind to know the future. And yet she knew. Somehow she knew.

The part about General Howe concerned him the most. How had she managed to be privy to Howe's state of mind?

"She spoke freely," Bradford said. "She told me of Washington's plans to make winter camp at Valley Forge."

"Indeed?" Hurlberry leaned forward.

"And apparently the rebel army means to undergo some arduous training during that time."

"They will need more than a winter's training to achieve competency. How did the Indian spy know of this?"

"If she were a spy, why divulge such information to me?" Bradford countered.

"I take it you were quite persuasive, Captain. What else did she tell you?"

"That the training would be conducted under the direction of a man titled Baron von Steuben."

"Steuben? Never heard of the man." Hurlberry sat back and twined his fingers together.

"How do you know she spoke the truth?"

"We won't. Not till winter." It did not escape Bradford's notice that the information Miss San Martin had provided was of limited use at the moment.

"How odd," Hurlberry murmured. "And yet, after all this, you obtained no confession?"

"There was naught to confess," Bradford repeated.

"Confident of this, Captain? I wonder that she did not employ her powers of seduction upon you, eh?"

Bradford did not reveal that it was he who had played the role of seducer. Instead, he said, "That concludes my report, Major."

Hurlberry bristled. "It is an extremely wanting report, Captain. Your performance has been most disappointing. I expected more of you. Given your lineage, I expected much more of you."

Bradford felt his anger rising from the depths of his gut. If the major alluded to his lineage one more time…

"You may redeem yourself to some extent, Captain. The rebels under the command of Brigadier General Wayne have been harassing our rear column. We have communiqués that the rebel has secluded himself two miles southwest of Paoli, presumably awaiting reinforcements, but we have been apprised by reliable informants that the rebel officer Maxwell is on the opposite side of the Schuylkill. If we act with speed, Maxwell cannot support his fellow officer in timely fashion from across the river. Moreover, it appears Washington himself makes for Parker Ford on the same side of the river as Maxwell. The river will run red before Maxwell and the other rebels realize what has happened. Major General Grey will lead the effort."

"And it is worth the effort to rid ourselves of a handful of rebels?" Bradford asked.

"Should we not concentrate on the greater goal of taking Philadelphia before winter?"

Hurlberry snickered. "The very words of your father. Do you lack the courage, Captain?"

Damn the man. Did he crave drawing pistols at dawn? But General Howe had made it clear how he felt about duels.

"I will report to General Grey, then."

"Yes, you had best, Captain."

* * * *

Major General Grey had comprised a brigade of nearly two thousand for the raid. The loyalists in the area had provided them with detailed intelligence of the Americans.

"Do you not think it a glorious strategy by General Grey to use only the bayonet?" asked Captain John **André** as he rode up to Bradford on his horse.

"The men are ready," Lieutenant Willoughby informed Bradford.

John continued, "These rebels, these hunters of squirrels, admittedly have good aim from a distance. But against the close range of steel, they are as helpless as babes. And as we are striking in the dead of night, firing would discover us to the enemy, hide them from us, kill our friends and produce a confusion favorable to the escape of the rebels and perhaps our own disgrace. By not firing, we shall know the foe to be wherever fire occurs. A charge ensures his destruction, and, amongst the enemy, those in the rear would fire against whoever fired in front.

They should destroy their own men."

Bradford noticed the eyes of his friend were alive with an ambitious gleam.

"In truth," John said, "I was afeared that the good general would see no command, but at last his time has come – and mine."

"You will no doubt attain your rank of major forthwith," Bradford assured him, listening with half an ear. His mind would not rid itself of Miss San Martin. He wished he could share John's exuberance, but he found himself wondering how Miss San Martin was faring and regretting that he had not accompanied her to her home. Though she had never made mention of where she resided, she seemed to have no fear of venturing alone. Perhaps she was a wandering gypsy. He knew so little of her. Yet he was incredibly drawn to her.

And it was more than a craving of flesh for flesh, though

that was a significant part. His loins ached with want and desire when he recalled the feel of her body beneath his. Soft. Supple. Womanly. The savory essence between her legs. The delicate folds that hid such a magnificent cunnie.

"And for that I must needs see action," John affirmed, breaking into Bradford's reverie. "Indeed, I am grateful for the entire war. There is naught more disastrous to the career of a soldier than peace."

This mission came at a fortunate time, Bradford decided. It would help remove Miss San

Martin from his thoughts and force his mind to the task at hand.

"Ah, Kerry."

It was his father.

"Your men are ready?" the general asked him.

After having served nearly a decade in the same army, his father should know that such a question was unnecessary.

"They are anxious to see combat, having missed the opportunity four days ago," Bradford informed him.

The general nodded. "I have no doubt we will put away the rebel nuisance. Wayne may be homegrown in these parts, but we have the aid of several local Tory farmers to serve as our guides."

"Here we go, and there they go," Bradford repeated the password that the Tories had provided them.

"If we are successful in capturing Philadelphia, then we will have taken an important step toward ending this wretched civil war. Mayhap the rebels will lay down their arms and become our brothers once more."

"She intimated we would be in Philadelphia by winter," Bradford murmured, recalling

Miss San Martin's words and reference to Washington at Valley Forge.

"Eh? The Indian? How fares Miss Lipps? Rather odd but interesting young woman, I must say," his father remarked.

"I hope well. I let her go…to the great consternation of Major Hurlberry. Any fool could see she was no rebel spy."

"Shall I have a word with the major?"

"No," Bradford said quickly. "Pray, do not."

"But the major is not one to tolerate, shall we say, consternation."

"Aye, but it be no concern of yours. It is a matter betwixt myself and the major."

"Very well," the general relented, but he did not appear too confident. "Should you need me, however…"

"I will not," Bradford emphasized for him, then wished he had not spoke quite so harshly.

But any interference by the general would only serve to further incense Hurlberry.

"Her name was Pauline San Martin," said Bradford, changing the subject. "Miss Lipps was a name she assumed while undertaking her, er, performances."

"Intriguing. Shall we see her again?"

"No, I think not."

And silently Bradford added the word *alas.*

Chapter Seventeen

Pauline trudged along where Route 1 ought to have been. She should be elated that Captain Bradford had let her go. Instead she felt sad. Had fled from the cabin because she worried if she stayed a second longer, she would not want to leave. And what if the captain were to change his mind later? She would have kicked herself then. But it was also the strength of her emotions when she was with Bradford that worried her. It was as if she had fallen in love with him.

She touched her hand where he had last placed his lips. Such a simple gesture, and it sent her heart through somersaults as if she were some giddy schoolgirl again.

Christ, what was the matter with her? Did she have the Patty Hearst syndrome where the captive falls for her captor? Was it because she felt scared and lonely and he was the only person she could connect with? The only one she felt safe with, despite the threat of being hung as a spy?

Where was she going? She had been walking aimlessly for hours. Who would she run into out here on these unfamiliar roads? She should probably head back to the Visitor Center.

There might be a portal of some sort in that area. She needed to do a more thorough search. Walking with no destination made no sense.

But back at the Visitor Center would be the British army. At least for the next day or two. Pauline went through her mind. If she had done her striptease on the seventeenth of September, then today was the twentieth. And the British would head to Philadelphia on the twenty-first, leaving her alone to explore the mysterious battlefield and possibly find a way back home. There would only be a minor skirmish between the Americans and British before the latter began their march. A skirmish known as the Paoli Massacre.

She felt a little sick at the thought. The Paoli Massacre was a part of history. Not pretty history for the Americans. The British would attack the unsuspecting Americans in the dead of night with a force of five thousand men, triple the number of American soldiers, under the command of General Grey – dubbed "No Flint" Grey because he would order his men to remove the flints from their guns prior to the attack. The poor Americans would be the only ones to discharge their guns, thus illuminating their presence to the British.

Perhaps the massacre need not happen if word reached the Americans. She felt a sense of responsibility in knowing what was to come. Or was it better not to tamper with history? Paoli was a blip among all the battles. Thought it became a rallying cry at the Battle of Germantown for the Americans, if the massacre never happened, the outcome of the war could hardly be different. The Americans would be better off without Paoli. She could singlehandedly prevent unnecessary bloodshed.

Paoli was up closer to Highway 202 – or rather, where 202 would be if it existed. It would be a good hike, but she could reach Paoli before the British did. She changed course and headed north. She was glad not to encounter anyone along the way and ate the provisions Bradford had given her. Though her boots were killing her, she kept up a brisk pace. She followed what she imagined would be Highway 322 north. But at some point she had to turn west.

Deciding it was better that if she did encounter someone, she looked like a man, Pauline tied her hair in a knot and pulled her shirt out to conceal her curves. It was dark when she came upon Willistown Township and had to ask directions. The night seemed to be on the side of the British, covering the moon with black clouds. She found the road the British would use on their march toward Paoli and walked along it for two more hours. She couldn't tell what time it was – sometime near midnight was her best guess – and she was no longer sure if she was ahead of or behind the British.

What if the Americans thought she was a crazy spy, too? Would they treat her better or worse than the British did?

No, they would see once they were attacked that she was right.

Up ahead Pauline could make out the lights of a town. She was hungry and thirsty, having finished her canteen of water. Needing to pee, Pauline decided to take care of nature's business in the bushes nearby. She unbuttoned her breeches, squatted, then realized she wasn't alone.

She stifled a scream upon seeing the prone body. It had been gutted with a bayonet. The British must be ahead of her. After quickly finishing up, Pauline jogged toward town. She saw the Admiral Warren Inne, a three-story Georgian with a row of windows neatly lining the first and second levels. Near it a blacksmith and an older man were grumbling to each other.

Pauline approached them. "Have the British passed by?"

"Aye," the blacksmith answered. "Asked me where the outer sentries for Anthony Wayne were."

"Wayne," spat the other man. "Bloody warned him that the British were coming. Dismissed me, he did."

Pauline dashed in the direction of the American camp. Maybe if Wayne received a second warning, he would reconsider. The British would come in from a northeasterly direction. Could she cut them off and reach the Americans first?

After a mile she could see the fires of the American camp shining through the night like little fireflies. The British had pulled off a near miraculous march. She hauled ass to the nearest makeshift hut she could see.

"The British! The British!" she called to one soldier who was sitting in front of his campfire warming a late-night dinner, using his bayonet as a cooking instrument.

Suddenly shots cracked the air. It was the last American picket firing at the British. It was too late.

The soldier turned his confused gaze from Pauline to where the shots had come from.

"Get up, for Chrissake!" Pauline yelled at him, nervously filling the pistols Captain Bradford had given her with the gunpowder and bullet. It wouldn't do much against the onslaught of bayonets, but it was all she had.

Then a vidette ran into the camp screaming, "Up men, the British are on you!"

A moment. Then pandemonium.

Led by the light infantry, the British troops descended on the Americans with the speed of a blitzkrieg. With a shudder, she heard the cries and screams of the American soldiers as the deadly blades sank into their flesh. Many of the Americans had been sleeping and could barely recall where they were, let alone how they might grab their weapons and fight back. They were revealed and silhouetted by their very own campfires.

Grabbing a blanket, Pauline tore it into long strips. She

wasn't a soldier. Except for the pistols, she had no weapon. The only thing she could do was tend to the wounded. And there would be lots of those.

General Wayne was attempting to form his frightened troops into lines, but the Americans were running around confused as chickens with their heads cut off. Even those in retreat met with bayonets.

The 1st Pennsylvania militia fired one volley toward the British but by doing so revealed their position. The British were upon them in seconds.

"Wheel by subplatoons," General Wayne ordered, trying to push his men to their right in order to face the enemy and provide time for his troops to escape along with the four cannons in their possession.

Pauline bandaged one of the American soldiers lying on the ground, but the linen became harder to work with as it became saturated with blood.

Somewhere to the west, General Smallwood and the Maryland brigade were posted. But the British had attained too good a position, and a maddening frenzy had set in upon the Americans. Colonel Richard Humpton's 2nd Brigade made the mistake of turning right when the rest of the army had turned left to escape. His troops walked right in front of the campfires and into the bayonets of the enemy.

"Mercy, I beg of you!" she heard one soldier cry before he was stabbed.

Pauline went from body to body, expecting a bayonet to slice through her own body at any moment. One British soldier stopped in front of her, and she considered reaching for a pistol. Her heart thumped madly during the three seconds they gazed at each other.

So this is how she was going to die.

But he must have mistook her for one of his own upon seeing her breeches and moved on.

Oh God, oh God, oh God. She could have died with relief. But she pressed on before she could think too long on that. Her arms pumped mechanically and furiously, hindered by the violent shaking of her fingers, as her ears tried to shut out the screams that filled the night air.

The 42nd British Regiment began setting fire to the huts to chase out the soldiers inside, but some of the frightened Americans chose to be burned alive rather than face the bayonet.

"What are *you* doing here?" came a hoarse shout.

Pauline looked up, her heart leaping at the sight of Captain Bradford.

"I was wrong," he said with a frown that wrenched her heart. "Major Hurlberry was right. You are a rebel spy."

"No! I swear!" Pauline replied, but her realization that it was going to be hard to explain herself now must have come across like guilt, for the captain's face was twisted with … pain? Anger? Betrayal?

"This is no place for a woman," he said.

A shot, and his horse reared onto her hind legs, throwing Bradford to the ground. Pauline ran to him and saw him clutching his shoulder. Blood seeped through his fingers. She looked up and saw the wild eyes of a young American. The soldier grabbed a rifle that lay on the ground. It must have been a British rifle, for it had a bayonet fixed to it. He charged toward Bradford. In an instant the bayonet would be buried in Bradford's stomach.

Without thinking, Pauline whipped out her pistol and fired.

The gunpowder scorched her hand, and she dropped it.

But the bullet had found its mark. The American soldier's eyes widened. He staggered. Then crumpled to the ground.

Pauline stared at the body. For seconds that lasted an eternity, she felt as if she couldn't move. She turned to Captain Bradford, saw him grimace in pain, and the numbness in her body faded enough for her to move.

"We have to stop the bleeding," she said to him, helping him to his feet.

"Nay, pay no heed," he commanded. "You must leave. It is not safe here."

Just then Lieutenant Willoughby rode up. "Captain, I saw you fall...."

Bradford grabbed the reins of his horse with his good arm. "Take Miss San Martin. Take her to safety."

"But you're hurt."

"Do as I command."

The lieutenant hesitated, then offered Pauline a hand up onto his horse. Remembering her last mount of a horse, the captain assisted her up.

"Take hold of his waist," he directed her. "We will dispense with formalities for the time being."

With some difficulty, he mounted his own horse.

"You should have that tended to," Pauline said.

"I will," he assured her.

Her heart soared at the gaze he fixed on her. The anger from before was gone. For a moment, she had thought he despised her. But it was clearly not the case now.

Lieutenant Willoughby urged his horse forward, and they headed back toward the Admiral Warren. Behind them, smoke filled the night air. Men ran in all directions. Some advancing.

Others fleeing. Occasional gunfire. But constantly the sound of steel meeting flesh, a strange, dull sound. Sometimes like a melon being sliced at harvest. And the agonizing wail of death descending.

"Wait. I need to get off," Pauline begged.

"But we have not arrived, " Willoughby protested.

"Now!"

She scrambled off the horse, fell into the nearest bush, and hurled.

* * * *

"I say we convene a tribunal to try Miss San Martin as a spy posthaste."

Major Hurlberry's words came as if from the end of a tunnel. Pauline heard the words "tribunal" and "spy," but all she could think of was the look of shock in the soldier's eyes as he fell to the ground. He might have been merely wounded. She should have checked. She had been too afraid to check.

Against the shadows thrown upon the wall of the Admiral Warren's attic by the two lone candles on the table, Major Hurlberry had an eerie appearance. Pauline sat before the small wooden table, her arms wrapped about her as if to ward off the cold, though she felt nothing.

Neither cold nor heat.

"I will not allow it," came a voice from the entrance.

Bradford! Pauline gasped with relief. He was alive. Her eyes searched him and found that he had had his shoulder bound, the left half of his coat draped over the injury. The rest of him looked fine, unharmed, and very much alive. She felt her numbness begin to melt away.

"I do believe I misheard you, Captain," the major snarled, "for you did *not* make a statement contrary to mine."

"I repeat it for you then. I will not allow it," replied the captain, not backing down.

"She did save Captain Bradford," Willoughby offered. "I saw it with my own eyes."

"How convenient," the major said, unconvinced. More footsteps came over the threshold. The major greeted the new arrivals. "Ah, Captain André, General Grey."

Pauline turned to look and gasped. It was like seeing a ghost. A dead man walking. Yet he was very much there.

With smooth cheekbones and a slender build, Captain John André, a young man of seven of twenty, had features of delicately carved porcelain. His dark complexion testified to his years as a soldier, but his aristocratic brow, clean-shaven face, and perfectly powdered hair revealed his true status. For some reason Pauline had always pictured him as a short man, but Captain André stood at a respectable height of five feet and nine inches. All in all, it was easy to see why a Connecticut militiamen would later remark that Captain André was the "handsomest man I ever laid eyes on."

Yet despite his capable build and intellectual air, there was something about him that made one almost want to bring him to one's bosom and shelter him tightly there. Was it because she sensed a boy still growing beneath that visage of a man? Or because she knew the ugly fate that would greet so pretty a neck? She felt a little saddened, as one feels when the blossoms of the trees have fulfilled their promise and are cast toward the ground at the end of spring. It was too fair a life to be extinguished in the failed attempts of one Benedict Arnold.

Behind André stood an older man wearing the most

magnificent uniform Pauline had yet seen. The broad lapels of his double-breasted coat were folded back to reveal the rich inner fabric. He wore gloves and gold buttons down his sleeves. His face was long, and he had dark, prominent eyebrows. She realized she must be looking at Sir General Charles Grey, the 1st Earl Grey, whose son, the 2nd Earl Grey, would become Prime Minister and have a tea named after him.

André approached Bradford. "I heard you were wounded, Kerry."

The young captain's eyes alighted on Pauline. "Who is this?"

"Miss Pauline San Martin," Bradford replied. "She saved me from certain death during the battle."

"A rebel spy," Hurlberry corrected. "Captain Bradford, I fear, is not unprejudiced."

Bradford took a step toward Hurlberry, and Pauline thought that if Bradford had a glove in hand, he would have smacked the major across the face.

"Hold your peace," General Grey commanded. "Major, we have executed a most successful assault on our enemy and prepare to march on Philadelphia tomorrow. For what purpose do you request my attention?"

"For this," said Hurlberry, pointing his long, crooked finger at Pauline. "I have reason to believe her a rebel spy. We found her amidst our soldiers at Brandywine. Captain Bradford was derelict in his duties and allowed the prisoner to escape. That we should discover her here proves that she meant to convey to the rebels intelligence regarding our plans."

"I meant no—" Pauline began before she was cut off by

179

Bradford.

"Silence," he told her. "Speak not a word."

He turned to the general. "I have no cause to believe her a spy."

"She killed a rebel solider," Lieutenant Willoughby added. "One who would surely have run a bayonet through Captain Bradford."

General Grey looked appreciatively upon Bradford. "Your valor on the field was exemplary, Captain Bradford. Your company fought well. But I fail to understand this matter with Miss... Miss..."

"Miss San Martin," Bradford supplied.

"Yes. Why was there a woman amidst the battlefield?"

"She is a rebel spy," the major reiterated for the umpteenth time. "We must deal a swift punishment that the rebels and those with rebel sympathies might know His Majesty's Army tolerates no spies."

"You have no proof of her spying," Bradford said.

"Had you fulfilled your duty properly, we would have had ample proof," the major returned.

The general frowned, clearly not happy with having to deal with the situation, especially when he wanted to bask in the glow of a lopsided victory.

"Major, with due respect," said André, "I have never known Kerry – Captain Bradford – to falter in his orders."

"His conduct surprised me as well, Captain André."

She could tell the major had no affinity for John André either. She itched to tell the general her side of the story, but she didn't want to upset Bradford.

"I will think on the matter," General Grey pronounced. "We will keep her here for now. Lieutenant Willoughby may keep watch of her."

"Perhaps we ought to have someone from a different company stand guard," Hurlberry suggested.

"You do not trust Lieutenant Willoughby?"

"I do not trust those under the command of Captain Bradford."

"This is a solemn matter," the general considered, running a hand along his jaw. "Very well. Captain André, direct one of the men from the 2nd to stand guard until I have determined the proper course of action."

Pauline watched as the men filed out of the attic. Captain Bradford, gripping his arm, approached her.

"Worry not," he assured her. "You will not hang. I pledge my word."

Major Hurlberry stood on the threshold, awaiting Captain Bradford. Bradford walked up to Hurlberry and stood toe-to-toe with the man, his stare boring into the elder officer until the major coughed uncomfortably and stepped aside. Pauline watched as the door closed behind them, leaving her alone.

Chapter Eighteen

W e hereby convene the Council of His Majesty's Army to attend the charges levied upon one Miss Pauline San Martin of spying and treason against the Crown."

Hands shackled in irons, Pauline stood in the middle of the main room of the Admiral Warren before five senior officers of His Majesty's Army, all sitting behind a long oak table. Covered in dried blood from Paoli, she looked a dreadful mess. Even the worst criminals in the twenty-first century were allowed to change into suits before their trials. But she was not in the twenty-first century. She was in the eighteenth century during a time of war. Habeas corpus and all the rights she would have been granted in her time were suspended or nonexistent.

"How plead you, Miss San Martin?"

"Not guilty," Pauline responded, but it didn't come out at all as confident and defiant.

"Major Hurlberry, you may present your case."

The major stood at attention, utilizing all five foot ten inches to tower over Pauline. "The spy was found on the seventeenth of September in an abhorrent attempt to seduce the soldiers of

His Majesty's Army, employing every wicked feminine wile and some that I hesitate to describe.

It would shock the modesty of any gentle soul."

Despite the gravity of her situation, Pauline couldn't help

wonder if the major was sex deprived and needed a good lay to dislodge the stick up his ass.

"When confronted, she revealed knowledge of our casualties – information that was privileged among officers," Hurlberry continued, reading from his notes. "And by Captain Bradford's very own assertion, she made mention of a possible alliance between the rebels and France. I commanded Captain Bradford to obtain from the spy all that she knew, but I regret to report that the captain fell woefully short of his orders. It is my belief that the spy has used her powers of seduction and tampered with his better judgment."

More like the other way around, Pauline thought to herself. She glanced up at the judges, the men who would determine her fate, searching for a sympathetic eye, a kindred soul. But they all wore stoic faces, and one seemed to nod exuberantly at the major's testimony.

The major wrapped up his presentation. "The Council should find Miss San Martin guilty and consider the only sentence appropriate to a spy – death by hanging."

The eldest of the officers turned to Bradford. "Captain, you have requested to defend the alleged spy. What have you to present?"

Never had she seen so regal a man, Pauline decided as she looked upon Captain Bradford, his hair perfectly coiffed and powdered, a new coat upon his broad shoulders, his boots polished and gleaming. She wished he would glance her way, lend her a reassuring smile, but he addressed the officers of the Council.

"I admit," he began, "that I, too, had suspicions that Miss San Martin might be in the service of the rebel army or even the French, but it quickly became evident that she is naught but an innocent bystander with the unhappy circumstance of having attempted to sell her wares, if you will, to the soldiers of my company."

"Her wares, Captain?" asked one of the officers.

"She is a dancer, but no ordinary dancer. As Major Hurlberry has intimated, she employs the arts of the fair sex to excite and titillate in exchange for money. In that she differs little from the prostitutes that abound in our camp."

"What of her singular knowledge of military intelligence?"

"Miss San Martin has been remarkably forthcoming with what she knows and bears intelligence of both our army as well as that of the rebels. But I beseech you, why would she offer up such knowledge if she knew it would condemn her to death?"

"Did she offer it freely?"

"Not all. Once she became aware that Major Hurlberry wished to hang her as a spy, she ceased to speak to me as once she did. I am, however, confident that she hides little from me. Contrary to what Major Hurlberry would have you believe, I fulfilled my duty and wrested from her all that I needed to know."

"You are sure of this, Captain?"

"I am."

"Pray, how can you be sure?"

"Allow me to demonstrate."

Pauline's heart started pounding, faster than the beat of a hummingbird's wing, it seemed. What in the world did Bradford mean by that? She watched as he approached her. The expression on his face was unreadable to her.

"The major would have you believe that Miss San Martin seduced me to her advantage,"

Captain Bradford said. He stood right next to her and ran the back of his hand along her cheek.

"But the truth is quite the opposite."

She wanted to jerk away from his touch but couldn't for some reason. She felt glued to the spot. Bradford had some plan, some strategy that she couldn't understand, but there was no reason to doubt him ... just yet.

"While Miss San Martin may be no virginal Pamela," Bradford continued, taking a step into her personal space. She could feel his body heat behind her, and it made her skin come alive.

"Her resistance was not half what that worthy heroine conveyed."

Turning her head to him, she hissed, "What are you saying, exactly?"

He grabbed her chin and pointed it back toward the Council. Her heart began pounding as his hand slid down her throat. He kissed her on the neck.

"She is a sexual creature," he explained to the Council, "and once aroused, desperate to spend."

Pauline sucked in her breath. She couldn't believe what he had just said – in front of five older men. In front of Major Hurlberry! Bradford's hand slid into her shirt and cupped a breast. This was outrageous. And yet her body warmed immediately to the closeness of his touch. Her nipple stretched into a hardened nub under his palm. He squeezed her breast, and that familiar aggravation pooled between her legs.

Oh God, this isn't happening, Pauline begged to herself. She wasn't quite sure where her bra had gone to, and the darks of her areolas were probably visible underneath the white shirt.

Bradford moved his hands to the shirt buttons and slowly undid them one by one.

"I'm not sure I agree with this defense strategy," Pauline whispered, but her conviction sounded weak even to her own ears.

"Shhh," he shushed as he pulled open the shirt and bared her breasts.

She shut her eyes, not wanting to see the reactions of the Council members. None of them said a word.

Standing behind her, Bradford palmed both breasts and began massaging them, pushing them together, pulling them apart, tugging at her nipples. And the best she could do while he mauled her breasts was whimper.

"Ah, that arouses you, Miss San Martin?" Bradford inquired.

Go to hell. Go to hell.

But the words wouldn't come out. She felt powerless against his caresses. He sucked on her neck, and each time he pulled on her tender flesh there, she felt a jolt right down to her pussy. This couldn't be happening, but she felt the telltale moisture forming in her nether region.

He pulled the shirt down a shoulder and caressed the area he exposed with his lips.

"Tell me how you surrendered to me," he murmured against her skin.

Her head snapped in his direction, her eyes wide. "Are you kidding?"

"She seems rather defiant, Captain," one of the officers remarked.

"Aye, she would make a show of resisting," Bradford replied, "but it does not endure for long."

To emphasize his point, he cupped her crotch, making her gasp. She tried to wriggle from his grasp, but he sawed his hand back and forth, pushing the fabric of the pants against her pussy lips, and her legs weakened.

"You surrendered to your desires, Miss San Martin. Confess it," Bradford urged.

The friction of the cloth against her made her moan. The ache, the itch was building. Her pussy clenched, signaling its desire.

He unbuttoned the breeches and pulled them down her thighs to provide the Council a view of her full frontal nudity. He slid a finger to her mons and rubbed her clitoris. Her breathing became difficult.

"Behold her wetness," Bradford said, holding up his finger.

Pauline looked on, horrified. The officers of the Council nodded. Bradford went back to fondling her clitoris.

"I await your confession, Miss San Martin," he reminded her.

She meekly shook her head. No. Not in front of these men. He responded by pushing a finger into her cunt. She nearly doubled over. Her toes curled. Her mind tried to rein in her traitorous body, and she pleaded to the Council with her eyes to stop the madness.

But they looked on, intrigued.

Bradford pushed two fingers into her hot and waiting cunt, making sure to rub her clitoris with every penetration. His other hand grabbed her breast, and she nearly lost all control. Her head fell back onto his shoulder as her hips began bucking against his hand.

He pulled away.

"No," she groaned.

"Confess it."

"Yes. Yes, I surrendered," she muttered, her entire body reverberating with agitation, needing his touch again.

"Louder, Miss San Martin."

"I surrendered," Pauline stated.

His hand returned. The caresses once again began fueling the yearning in her loins.

"Tell the Council how you craved my caress and how you desired me to ravish your body."

This was too embarrassing, but she was beyond the point of no return. Her body was an instrument, and Bradford the maestro.

"Yes, I desired it," she said.

His fingers attacked her clitoris. Her orgasm loomed within reach.

"I wanted...you...to ravish me," she said, every nerve in her body straining for that climax. "Ravish me."

She was so close. "Oh, yes. Fuck me."

So very close.

"Fuck me, fuck me, fuck me."

His fingers dug into her breast. Thrummed against her clit. Her orgasm erupted, and she convulsed in Bradford's hands, one long cry of relief followed by short, muted cries when he continued his caresses to eke out the last of her spasms. Then he finally withdrew his hand and brought it to her lips. She smelled the musky fragrance of her own come.

"Taste of yourself," he said into her ears.

Her lips parted, and he pushed his fingers into her mouth. It tasted tangy and not entirely disagreeable.

"And this, your honors," Bradford said, "marks only the beginning."

Chapter Nineteen

Pauline bolted upright. Her pulse was rapid. She looked about her and saw the attic of the Admiral Warren. It had been a dream. She had fallen asleep on the table. She hadn't gone before the tribunal. It had all been a dream. She drew in a haggard breath of relief.

There was a knock at the door, and Captain Bradford appeared.

"How do you fare, Miss San Martin?" he asked, closing the door behind him.

The tenderness in his voice made her want to fling herself into his arms, but she stayed where she was.

"Major Surlyberry allowed you to see the prisoner?" she asked, but her attempt at levity fell flat even to her own ears.

"Captain André is a friend of mine and has instructed the guard not to disturb us," Bradford explained. He walked up to her.

She knew the question he would ask her and could not bring herself to look him directly in the eye. She felt as if he had betrayed his trust. It had not occurred to her how much trouble Captain Bradford might have been in letting her go in the first place, and now she had placed him in an even worse situation.

"I do not fancy you came to Paoli for me," he remarked.

She dared to meet his gaze, needing to know if he condemned her for what she had done. "I thought I could prevent unnecessary bloodshed. I never meant to hurt anyone or put anyone in harm's way – especially you. I'm not a rebel spy."

"The decision to attack was determined whilst we were…away. How you come by your extraordinary knowledge exceeds my comprehension. But for sorcery—"

"I'm not a witch. I'm not a sorceress. I – oh, it doesn't matter. I don't believe it myself."

"You may not be a rebel spy, Miss San Martin, but your actions speak to treason."

Pauline looked down at her hands folded in her lap. "I'm sorry."

Bradford knelt down on a knee to look into her eyes. His gaze scanned her face. "For what purpose do you apologize?"

Tears pressed themselves against the back of her eyes, painful to hold back.

"I don't know," she mumbled.

He cupped her chin and turned her gaze toward his, but in the dimness of the attic, his eyes shone too brightly for her. She kept her lashes lowered, for if she looked him in the eye, she was likely to break down crying.

Bradford pressed his lips together grimly. "You have no need to apologize. Your actions were born of courage. That much was evident. You may be a rebel, but you are brave one, Miss San Martin."

She shook her head and looked at him in desperation. "I…I shot a man—"

Then she couldn't hold back. The sobs tore through her body, her tired mind unable to cope. Bradford enveloped her in his arms. The strength of his embrace, the comfort and protection of it, only made her cry harder. The tears streamed down her face and pooled onto his coat. He held her firmly until the sobs subsided into trembles and sniffles. She held on to the lapels of his coat, the sound of his heartbeat next to her ear a source of calm.

"I've made things worse for you. Major Hurlberry is madder than ever," she noted as she blinked away the last of her tears.

"To hell with Hurlberry," Bradford replied. "I will not see you hanged. I owe my life to you."

She didn't want him to defend her out of obligation. She wanted him to *care* about her, and when she glanced up at him, something in the way he looked at her made her hopeful. He stroked away a tear on her cheek with the back of his hand. Then his mouth dipped toward hers.

The kiss was gentle at first, covering her mouth the way his arms had held her. But it quickly became more demanding, more urgent. And she needed it, needed him. Her hands circled to the back of his neck, pressing him harder to her as the kiss deepened and became more impassioned. They devoured each other with their mouths, desperate to meld into one.

It might have been the stress of the situation, the fear for her future, that drove the intensity of feeling she had for Bradford. But she wanted him, desired him, needed him like no other. Like she would go mad without him. She clung to him tightly, pressed her body to his so hard it hurt.

"I haven't a sheath with me," he murmured against her lips, a little surprised by her passion.

"It doesn't matter," she answered back.

"Are you certain?"

Pauline responded by pushing her tongue toward the back of his throat. He groaned and wrapped his good arm around her waist, pulling her pelvis to him. She got up on her knees and worked her mouth voraciously over his, tasting of him thoroughly, as if he were her last supper.

"Lie back," she told him. With his bad shoulder, he wouldn't be able to be on top without straining himself.

As fast as she could, she unbuttoned his breeches. He had said they would not be interrupted, but who knew when Hurlberry would decide to return to glower some more at her.

His cock sprang toward her, beautiful and straight. There wasn't much time to marvel at it, but she couldn't resist putting her mouth over the head of it, lapping the underside with her tongue, swirling her tongue over the tip. Bradford swore beneath his breath as she pulled up. The top of his cock glistened with the wetness from her mouth.

After shedding her boots and breeches, she lowered herself on top of him. His cock – raw, unsheathed, naked – inside her felt amazing. The skin of his penis felt so soft and smooth. The ridges of the veins were sublime as her vaginal walls flexed tightly against him. She had slid so easily onto him, as if their bodies were meant to be together. She savored the feeling of him buried to the hilt in her before she began to rise and fall on his shaft.

Bradford grabbed a hip with his good arm and helped lift her up and pull her down. He bucked his hips against her in time to her motions, grimacing at times.

"Are you in pain?" Pauline asked with worry, thinking about his shoulder.

"God, no," he grunted and shoved his cock harder into her.

His thumb found her clitoris, and soon she was spasming on his cock, crying out, hoping the guard wouldn't rush in to see what was afoot. Bradford pushed himself into her with such force she thought she would bounce right off him, and then she felt his warm seed spilling into her, his legs trembling beneath her. She fell onto his chest, panting. His cock throbbed inside her pussy, and she wished their bodies could be joined like this forever.

* * * *

After they had dressed, Bradford held her in his arms on the floor of the attic, leaning against the wall. His shoulder throbbed with pain. He'd known the exertion would worsen it – he had lied when she had asked him if he was in pain – but he had wanted as much to be a part of her as she had of him. The feel of her flesh upon his cock had been wondrous, and he had been hard-pressed not to spend himself that instant. Even the memory of her hot, wet cunnie sheathing his cock made the blood flow faster to his loins.

She was remarkable in such numerous ways.

When he had first laid eyes on her on the battlefield of Paoli, his heart had plummeted. He felt betrayal, anger, and fear for her safety. The betrayal and anger were blown away by the shot she aimed at the rebel soldier. He could tell in an instant, by the depth of the shock in her eyes, that she had never fired a shot at anyone before. There was no time for gratitude then. That came later, as did admiration and another feeling he could ill describe.

She was an American sympathizer, but that made her no less brave. It took courage to want freedom. Courage to want it enough to fight for it. He would see her treated with the honor and justice she deserved. It was more than a quid pro quo on his part for saving his life. That she would turn arms against her own countrymen filled him with more than gratitude. It was hope. That she felt as strongly about him as he did her.

The door flew open and Captain André appeared.

"Forgive me, but I could wait no longer," John said after recovering from his surprise at finding his friend in a most familiar manner with the captive.

Bradford rose to his feet and assisted Miss San Martin to hers.

"I overheard Major Hurlberry with General Grey," John explained. "The man means to have your head."

"The affection Major Hurlberry bears for me is not lost upon me," Bradford replied wryly.

"Kerry, the major wishes to convene a tribunal on your conduct. At best, it would be thirty lashes for insubordination. At worst, a court-martial."

"No! He can't!" Miss San Martin protested.

The concern in her voice filled his heart. He drank in her lovely countenance and held her hand.

"Worry not," he told her. "The major has no influence upon me."

"Kerry, a word with you, if I may?" John asked.

After another reassurance to Miss San Martin, Bradford followed his friend outside.

"Major Hurlberry was quite vociferous in his statement to Grey," John said. He glanced away, then back at Bradford. "And were I not well acquainted with you, Kerry, I would think the major had merit to his claims."

Bradford detected some hesitancy in André. "Indeed?"

"Who is this Pauline San Martin?"

"A woman who saved my life."

"And did she mean to save it? These natives are unpredictable at best."

"She did not have to fire the pistol I gave her."

"You gave her a pistol?" André asked with eyes wide.

"She could have shot me instead," Bradford finished. "I thought to have Lieutenant Willoughby take her into safekeeping. Had I known she might fare better on the battlefield…"

"Major Hurlberry is quite convinced of her treachery."

"I don't bloody care," Bradford said with growing impatience, "if she took arms against us in every battle we have waged. She saved my life."

"And for that you feel you must save hers? And risk your advancement for it – nay, more than your advancement. Mark my words, a court-martial is what Hurlberry requested."

"And you are convinced the major will succeed in his application?"

André shook his head. "I have known you for many years, Kerry. I must say this is unlike you, to risk so much for a fancy."

Bradford looked at André. His friend knew less of him than he would have thought.

"I could not leave her to her fate," he explained. "And I would not be worthy of the rank of major were I not to do what honor would dictate."

By the frown on André's face, Bradford could tell his friend was not satisfied, but he no longer wished to spend time convincing John that he saw no other course of action for himself, even if it meant a poor end for both Miss San Martin and himself.

* * * *

"Inform the general I wish to speak to him," Bradford told the aide-de-camp.

As he waited, Bradford paced the floor outside the general's room in the inn. He clenched and unclenched his hands. For two hours he had turned over thought after thought and came up empty-handed. He was fairly certain General Grey would not stall the march to Philadelphia to try Miss San Martin, but the notion of marching the sennight with Miss San Martin as a prisoner, and perhaps installing her in a gaol when they reached Philadelphia, was not acceptable. How would she be treated? Would the army house her as it would the other prisoners of war?

"The general will see you," the aide-de-camp informed him.

Bradford hesitated, but he pushed himself through the door, feeling that facing the guns of the rebels would have been easier than this.

"I thought you at Paoli?" General Bradford remarked from the writing table. He turned around to look at his son, and his face paled upon seeing the sling. "You are injured."

"Only slightly," Bradford replied.

The general, never one to dote, leaving such sensibilities instead to his wife, accepted his son's statement. "The raid was successful?"

"We could not have hoped for better."

"And the purpose of your return, then?"

Alas, the general was not slow in thinking, Bradford thought to himself. He had not fully prepared how he would present the situation of Miss San Martin, as if he had hoped a solution might present itself miraculously to him before he came to see his father. For all the years he had served in the army, he had never once needed to ask the general a favor. He could not remember the last time he had asked anything of his father. As a younger man, he would simply choose to learn it himself – the hard way, if need be – and to hide his struggles.

"An unusual matter," Bradford began. It would not do to skirt the truth now, for his father would know that something was afoot. "Major Hurlberry would see Miss San Martin hanged as a rebel spy."

"Is she indeed a rebel spy, then?"

His jaw tightened. "She saved my life on the fields of Paoli. I will not see her harmed."

The general cocked an eyebrow. "Did she?"

Bradford let out a deep breath and decided to tell his father the whole of it: Major Hurlberry's assignment, what he was able to elicit from Miss San Martin during their time alone, how he let her go, and their meeting at Paoli. Surprisingly, he found relief in laying out the state of affairs to his father, though there was no knowing how his father would react. And Bradford dreaded his father's condemnation more than the wrath of Major Hurlberry.

Would the general be angered that his son had risked a promising career on a woman he barely knew? Would he be disappointed? Saddened? Bradford would have preferred his father's rage to sorrow. He did not think he could bear to know that he had broken his father's heart and dashed his longest held dreams. And yet he felt compelled to do just that by feelings he had not been able to sort out. By a force greater than he had ever thought to find in himself.

General Bradford considered the matter in silence.

"The circumstances are grave," he noted. "And I doubt a word from me will sway Major Hurlberry."

"I doubt even bending my knee to the major and begging his forgiveness would alter his stance," Bradford said through clenched teeth.

The general regarded his son. "You have your mother's pride and stubbornness."

"I have my mother's stubbornness, but your pride, sir."

General Bradford frowned. "Yes, that would be the case as well."

"I have a desire to bring the matter to Lord Cornwallis," Bradford announced. "And General Howe if need be."

"Perhaps we can convince Grey that there be a better solution," said the elder Bradford. "I have a plan."

Chapter Twenty

Early on a wet and rather chilly morning, the British set out for the Schuylkill, their destination Philadelphia. General Grey had completed the raid of last night with great success. His men had fallen upon the Americans with speed and agility and returned as promptly, not wasting a minute more than was necessary at Paoli.

Wayne had managed to save his cannons, but fifty-three of his men would die. Another seventy-one had been captured, and over one hundred were wounded. The British had seven wounded and four killed.

The locals would wake to find the hillsides seeped in blood and covered with the maimed and burnt flesh of humans. As the British had left camp, burial responsibilities fell upon the farmers, and since the land upon which the massacre occurred belonged to a Tory, the Americans were forced to bury the soldiers elsewhere. Of those captured, some had injuries so severe General Howe refused his surgeons permission to operate and would instead write a letter to Washington asking for American doctors to tend the wounded.

For better or worse, the delayed response of the American soldiers had been due in part to the fact that their guns, powder, and cartridges had been wrapped in cloth to prevent their getting wet in the rain. Four hundred thousand cartridges had been ruined by the rain on the nineteenth.

Colonel Humpton, whose troops had suffered the greatest losses at Paoli, would file charges against Wayne. A tribunal would eventually clear Wayne and acquit him with the "highest honor."

* * * *

Pauline stared at the long columns of soldiers as they marched toward the colonial capital. It occurred to her that she might be stuck forever in the eighteenth century. She didn't know how she'd gotten here, so there was no road map for how to get back. But at least she didn't have the hangman's noose hanging over her anymore.

And she had Captain Kerry Bradford at her side, safe and sound. That felt the best of all.

She had knotted her stomach in worry of him last night when she should have been thinking of how to get herself out of her own mess. Wracked with worry and guilt, she had chewed on all ten of her fingernails, all of which now had uneven edges that no manicure could save.

"General, thank you," Pauline said as she looked up at the elder Bradford upon his horse.

"My dear, you've no need to thank me a hundred times," the general responded. "Once will do."

"A hundred would not be enough, sir."

And she meant it. The general had even managed to procure a gown and petticoats for her. It wasn't the most attractive dress, and came up a little short for her, and it wasn't nearly as comfortable as wearing shirt and breeches, but she appreciated the gesture. Especially since it seemed she might be staying awhile in 1777. Who knew when and if she would find her way back home? And until she could, she would have to make the best of her situation.

And that included serving His Majesty's Army. She had to

believe, given her knowledge, that she could outsmart the British and preserve the integrity of history. And she was only too glad to be able to save her own neck and that of Captain Bradford, too.

To Major Hurlberry's consternation, General Bradford had approached General Grey and convinced the man that Pauline possessed information that could be of service to the British. At the least, what she had told Kerry needed to be validated. Until that time, they could neither confirm nor deny her guilt.

"Then what will you have us do with her?" Grey had asked.

"I shall make her my ward," General Bradford had declared.

Pauline had felt her heart filling with love for the man. She hoped with all her might that the inscription at the Brandywine Visitor Center museum was wrong.

The general had turned a kindly eye toward her. "It is the least I can do for saving my son's life."

"You will not be coerced into anything you do not wish to do," Captain Bradford had assured her when the general had stepped out with Grey. He lifted her chin. "Least of all by me."

She grasped his hand and wrapped her fingers tightly about it. "I'm okay with this."

He moved their hands to his lips, and Pauline felt her heart soar even as she lost herself in the depths of his gaze. His head lowered toward hers, and his lips brushed hers. It was a kiss filled with tenderness, fondness, and, she hoped, affection. She returned it with the strength of her own feelings until a cough at the door forced them reluctantly apart.

As she looked up at the grayish sky, reliving their last kiss,

Captain Bradford pulled his horse alongside Pauline and the general.

"Major Hurlberry's going to hate you for life," Pauline told Bradford.

"Better his wrath than the cat upon my back," Bradford replied.

"You sure about that?"

"Without a doubt."

An officer of proximate age to General Bradford rode up. The man had a sweeping brow and a round form. He wore his coat open, revealing his golden colored waistcoat and a wide sash across his torso.

"Ah, this must be the infamous Miss San Martin," the man said.

"Lord Cornwallis, it's an honor," Pauline said with a curtsy to the man who would be commander-in-chief and surrender to Washington at Yorktown, bringing an end to the American Revolution. Aligned with the Whig party in Parliament, General Charles Cornwallis had never favored going to war with the colonies but had accepted his post in His Majesty's Army nonetheless.

"I've read so much … I mean, I've heard so much about you," she corrected. "No worries – all good things. I've only heard good things about you. And I do mean it's an honor. Truly."

Lord Cornwallis glanced at General Bradford, who was looking at her with the same odd expression his son was prone to giving her. Pauline wondered if the senior Bradford would regret taking her into his protective custody.

"Your ward, Stephen," Cornwallis addressed General Bradford, "is most charming."

The two generals proceeded to have a private conversation. Pauline let out a breath and looked at Captain Bradford, who was suppressing a grin while shaking his head. He looked at her in her gown and boots with an appreciative sweep, and Pauline was glad to be able to appeal to him wearing something more feminine.

"Charming indeed," he murmured.

She felt her cheeks warm. She wondered what their relationship would be like from now on. Was their interlude in the cabin but a tryst? A fling?

"We shall have to procure a horse for you," Bradford noted.

"No, thanks," she responded. "Your father already offered. Horses make me nervous, and I make them nervous."

Captain Bradford swung off his horse. "Then I shall walk with you. It would not do for me to ride if you cannot."

"Even though I'm your prisoner?"

"You are a prisoner no longer."

"Are you always his chivalrous, Captain?" she asked with a smile. "You know, I'm not sure which I like better, your treating me like a princess – or like a strumpet."

Bradford lowered his voice. "I know your kind, Miss San Martin. You relish the latter, and upon the first tavern we encounter, be assured that I will have my way with you."

"Or I just might have my way with *you*," Pauline retorted.

"By all means, but only if you perform your *lap dance* for me."

They exchanged smiles and walked side by side. She took in a breath of air. It was crisp, fresher than the air she was accustomed to breathing. The sky seemed more expansive, its breadth spread as wide as her future now seemed.

MORE WICKED HOT EROTIC ROMANCES BY EM BROWN

Cavern of Pleasure Series
Mastering the Marchioness
Conquering the Countess
Binding the Baroness
Lord Barclay's Seduction

Red Chrysanthemum Stories
Master vs. Mistress
Master vs. Mistress: The Challenge Continues
Seducing the Master
Taking the Temptress
Master vs. Temptress: The Final Submission
A Wedding Night Submission
Punishing Miss Primrose, Parts I - XX

Chateau Debauchery Series
Submitting to the Rake
Submitting to Lord Rockwell
Submitting to His Lordship
Submitting to the Baron
Submitting to the Marquess
Submitting for Christmas

Other Stories
Claiming a Pirate